FEAR AT THE FERRIS WHEEL

A WHODUNIT PET COZY MYSTERY SERIES BOOK 3

MEL MCCOY

*S*arah Shores sat, dumbfounded, at Teek's Tiki Bar, staring at her empty mojito glass, which now rested forlornly on the bar top. She could still smell Officer Adam Dunkin's cologne lingering in the air beside her, where he'd been sitting before he received the phone call and hurried off on official police duty. Something about someone dying at the amusement park —an "accident."

She knew it could be much more than just an accident, if the past two incidents were any indication. Since arriving in Cascade Cove not more than a few weeks ago, the mysteries surrounding a washed-up landowner and a strangled food critic had kept her busy. In the back of her mind, she knew life wouldn't be getting back to normal any time soon.

"Have a good night," Sarah said to Teek, the muscular surfer dude who owned the bar, the only speakeasy tiki bar in the area—and the only one in all of the state of Florida, for all Sarah knew. His blond hair contrasted his tanned skin, and his biceps flexed as he grabbed a bottle of spirits from behind where he stood. She paid her tab with a smile, flicking strands of her long, brown hair out of her face. Her own skin was becoming tanned, now that she'd been here a few weeks—prior to leaving New York City, she'd been the definition of pale.

"Later, dudette," Teek said, then another bar patron waved him down and he hurried over to them, leaving her with the tail end of "Sweet Home Alabama" playing on the jukebox.

Sarah flung herself off the stool and hurried out of the bar, weaving through the people who had accumulated in the place in the short time she'd been there. Once out of the bar, she rushed south along the boardwalk, toward where the small amusement park was situated.

Up near where the Ferris wheel loomed, she spotted the flashing lights. Ambulances and police cars. The cavalry had arrived.

At the entrance to the amusement park, she hurried past the multitude of nearly empty food vendors.

Cotton candy, hot dogs, and soft pretzels could be seen in her peripherals, and she ignored the delicious smells.

A few people in matching attire rushed past her, looking a bit confused. Sarah figured they were all park employees, as they sported the same khaki pants and tucked-in blue polos embroidered with the park's insignia on the right breast pocket.

Then, she passed a section that hosted a mix of games. A man at the water gun game looked bored without any players, arms crossed over his blue polo. At the ring toss, Sarah noticed a woman tapping incessantly on her phone. Perhaps she was texting a friend about what was happening. Either way, like the water gun operator, she was probably stuck at her station until her shift ended. Of course, Sarah knew she likely wouldn't have anyone interested in tossing a plastic ring over a bottle, with what was happening elsewhere in the park.

Closing in on the flashing lights, Sarah scanned the crowd of people near the Ferris wheel. People of all ages were gathered around, murmured words floating about with the smell of fried foods.

Finally, near the Ferris wheel where the ambulance was parked, she had a closer view, and could make out some of the hushed voices.

"I can't believe it," an elderly man said. "How did they die?"

"I heard it was a heart attack," replied another.

Sarah weaved through the crowd and spotted the stretcher being pushed into the back of the ambulance. She only saw a pair of tan shoes but couldn't tell if they were men's or women's footwear. She squinted, but then someone got in her way, obstructing her view.

A man in an EMT uniform was shaking his head at a colleague, but Sarah had already known the person had died. Perhaps their attempts at reviving them had been exhausted.

Then she saw Adam, her police officer friend. One of her closest friends and allies, she'd known him since they were teenagers, when Sarah would come down to visit her grandparents every summer in Cascade Cove. Now, over the past few weeks, they had been getting closer than ever—a fact that made her unsure if she'd ever want to leave Cascade Cove, though she had responsibilities back in the city. She'd agreed to extend what originally was supposed to be a two-week visit to stay for the whole summer to help out at the boutique. In the back of her mind, there was more to it than that. She'd miss Adam too much if she didn't stay awhile longer.

Gazing at Adam, she saw that he held a tiny notebook in his hand, and was jotting something down into it. She wanted to waltz up to him and get to the bottom of what was happening, but he seemed busy talking with a few amusement park employees.

Out of the corner of her eye, Sarah noticed a young man in a black hoodie, wearing a bright-red baseball cap. He was staring straight at her, his eyes boring into her.

She turned to look, but by then, he was eyeing the scene near the ambulance, hands fidgeting as he watched.

Turning back toward the Ferris wheel, with bright lights flashing all around, Sarah got the same sense that she was being watched. Out of her peripherals, she confirmed her suspicions—the man in the red hat was focused again on her, studying her.

But when she turned again to get a better look at him, he was gone.

"What the heck," she muttered, stepping toward where the man had been.

Why was this man acting so suspicious? And why in the world had he been staring at her?

Rushing through the crowd, Sarah looked off to her right, down a section of park that was lined with food stalls and games. There were a few shed-like buildings, painted in all sorts of shades of blue and red, accenting the off-white paint that flecked from the incessant Florida sunshine. This part of the park was vacant, since everyone had congregated near where the death had occurred. But where had the mystery man gone?

She stepped cautiously, scanning the lifeless path before her.

There! Toward the end of the line, she spotted the red hat poking out from around a corner. The man was eyeing her again.

She took off at a jog, knowing it was unwise to run toward a stranger in a desolate section of the park this late at night, but she put all discretion aside—the only thing on her mind was getting a chance to talk to the guy. Perhaps he'd seen what had actually happened to the person who died. Maybe he was shaken up after telling the cops what he'd seen. Sure, she could ask Adam, but that would have to wait. And the last thing Sarah wanted to do was wait. Her curiosity was getting the better of her.

She reached the corner at which the man had been, but when she rounded it, no one was there.

Where had the mystery man gone? And what did he know about the person who had perished here at the amusement park?

Sarah was itching to find out.

CHAPTER 2

The next morning, Sarah was finishing up stocking one of the shelves at Larry's Pawfect Boutique, her grandpa's namesake pet store. The mornings and early afternoons were typically spent helping out at the boutique, and today was no different. Despite all the goings on, particularly the death at the amusement park the previous night, it was still business as usual at her family's shop.

She caught motion out of the corner of her eye and remained crouched as she turned her head toward the counter. There, she spotted her cousin, Emma, who was lounging and tossing a tennis ball up into the air. A moment later, Emma caught the ball, then lobbed it back up toward the ceiling again.

Sarah let out a long breath, still glancing at her

cousin. As usual, Emma had her blonde hair tied up in a ponytail. Both she and Emma had been close during their childhoods, visiting their grandparents over the summer in Cascade Cove. Over the years, they'd drifted apart as their summers together became much shorter—typically two weeks, rather than the three months they'd enjoyed in their youth. Adulthood brought more responsibility, though Emma had opted to move down with her grandparents, leaving the rest of her family up north.

Picking up an empty box that sat beside her, Sarah rose and took one final look at her handiwork. The squeaky toys she'd just put out made her smile. Each one was a different type of food—her favorites being the watermelon slice, banana, carrot, and pumpkin. She couldn't get over the cutesy eyes that adorned each one.

She carried the box toward her cousin, who was still playing with the ball. "Don't you have any work to do, Emma? Maybe the website?"

"Not today."

"Oh? Why's that?"

"I know it's not even noon, but I'm taking a well-deserved break, and you should too."

Sarah set the box on the counter and gave her cousin one curt nod. "You're probably right."

In truth, Sarah felt she could use a break. She

thought back to the previous night. Unable to track down the man in the red hat, and without the chance to speak to Adam in person, she had left the amusement park with a sense of unease and frustration. She'd tried to text and call Adam after getting back to the apartment, but he had yet to get back to her—she knew he was probably busy, though it was unlike him to ignore her. She couldn't shake the strange man in the red cap who'd been staring at her—he had been acting very suspicious, and had even evaded her when she attempted to talk with him. If what had happened was a murder, maybe the man had information that could help her nab the killer. Though, she realized she was getting ten steps ahead of herself. For all she knew, it could have been an accident, though her intuition told her otherwise...

The jingle of tags on a collar broke into her thoughts, and Sarah saw Winston approach them. The corgi spent a lot of time in the boutique with them since she'd adopted him—he was always eager to greet all the customers and their pets. Of course, his constant companions—an eighty-pound yellow lab named Rugby and a Persian cat called Misty—were off in another part of the boutique or the upstairs apartment, as usual.

Sitting up, Emma ceased lobbing the tennis ball into the air, instead favoring the time-tested method of flipping it to and fro from one hand to another. Winston's gaze quickly locked onto it, and so his head bobbed back and forth as he eyed the ball.

"Wanna play, boy?" Emma asked.

The corgi's gaze was still fixed on the ball.

Emma tossed it toward the middle of the store. Moments later, it clanged off the display Sarah had just stocked.

Winston darted toward the ball, retrieved it, and proudly trotted back toward the counter. He dropped it lazily, and it rolled toward where Emma's feet rested on the ground.

Emma ignored it. "So, Sarah, why were you out so late last night?"

"I told you already. Went to Teek's, Adam got a phone call about a person dying at the amusement park, then I went there and—"

"Oh yeah, the guy in the black hoodie and red hat. That's weird how he was staring at you."

Sarah nodded. Weird *and* unsettling. She couldn't shake that feeling of being watched.

"Maybe he's the killer," Emma said.

Sarah glanced at her cousin, wanting to say something about jumping to conclusions, but she bit her tongue. "I just want to talk to the guy. See what he knows. I don't even know if the person who died was a man or a woman. I don't know anything."

"Too bad you couldn't talk to him last night. You need to get faster at running, so you can catch up next time."

"I'm not as fast as I used to be."

Emma shrugged. "Such is life. But don't worry about it...I'll ask around and see if anyone's heard about it through the grapevine."

"Good idea."

"So...it's been another week, Sarah. Have you thought about what we talked about before, about you moving here, to Cascade Cove, and helping us run the boutique?"

"You mean, help you run the boutique when Grandpa gets busy with the online orders?"

"I have a feeling I'll be running the online orders. Have you seen how bad he is with technology?"

Sarah stifled a chuckle. "He can at least run a register."

Both Sarah and her cousin laughed at the memory of Emma trying to teach Grandma how to run the register. Sarah knew the endearing woman would understand how to use it properly eventually, but she'd been unwilling to accept that you couldn't just hit No Sale while ringing out an actual sale. Perhaps she'd never acquiesce and would simply ignore Emma's guidance in regard to "modern" technology.

Emma added, "Though, even though Grandpa can run the register, he's terrible with computers. He needs a manual to even turn one on."

"Oh, be nice, Emma."

Sure, Emma was a spitfire and her humor could be taken the wrong way, but Sarah adored her spunky personality.

Emma giggled. "You know as well as I do, it took me three years to teach him how to input inventory into the computer properly. I'm sure it will take me another three to show him how to do online orders. See, we really do need your help."

Leaning down, Emma grabbed the tennis ball, then threw it once again. Winston raced after it as it bounced toward the front door, leaving Sarah and Emma alone for a moment.

"And besides," Emma continued, "you even said that you love it here and wish you could be with us all the time."

"I still have a job, you know."

"So, quit."

"I can't just quit."

Emma's smile was breezy. "Yes, you can. It's easy. You just pick up the phone and say, 'I quit.' Done."

Sarah shifted her weight, considering the crazy idea her cousin had just suggested. How could she advise her to just quit her job? She'd spent years advancing in her teaching career—she couldn't just give up on all of that. Then, she thought about how much she enjoyed being with her family on the beach. It sure beat the city. Sarah took a deep breath, trying her best not to even entertain the idea of quitting her job. "Even if I do that," Sarah said, keeping her voice calm, "I don't think Grandpa is real keen on big ol' Rugby running amok in the boutique."

"Are you kidding? He loves that dog!"

Before Sarah could reply, the sound of Larry's voice came echoing from upstairs through the vent. "Rugby!"

Sarah and Emma both perked up.

"Bad dog!" came Larry's voice again.

"Uh-oh," Sarah said. "What now?"

Emma shrugged.

In the next moment, stomping footsteps came down the stairs into the boutique.

Sarah spun to face the door that led to the upstairs apartment and saw Larry burst through the door. His face was beet red, which complemented his Hawaiian shirt. He used a thin index finger to push his glasses up on his nose, then ran a hand through his curly, gray hair, clearly distraught.

"What happened?" Sarah asked, approaching her grandpa.

Larry held up a pair of his boxer shorts and Sarah's eyes went wide. There, in the backend of the underwear, was a gaping hole where the fabric had been torn off.

Behind her, Emma snorted, trying to hold back laughter. And even though Sarah felt terrible about Larry's destroyed undergarments, she couldn't help herself from bursting out a laugh.

"It's not funny, girls." Larry's face grew a brighter shade of red.

"We're not laughing, Grandpa," Sarah said, now trying extra hard to restrain herself. "I'm sorry. I'll buy you new ones."

Larry's shoulders hunched slightly as he brought the boxers down to his side. "But these are my lucky pair. I've had them for twenty-five years!"

"All the more reason to take up Sarah's offer," Emma said.

Muted thuds sounded from behind Larry, and Sarah spotted Rugby gallivanting down the steps like a clumsy ball of fury. In a flash, the yellow lab rushed up behind Larry and snagged the boxers again, taking off back up the steps.

"Rugby!" Larry shouted and ran after him, with Winston hot on his heels.

"Those boxers are toast," Emma said, shooting Sarah a sideways glance. "It's game-over for them."

Sarah spotted the abandoned tennis ball on the floor near Emma's feet. "I'll say. Game, match, set."

Emma followed her gaze and eyed the ball, and their shared snorted laughter echoed through the boutique, drowning out the sounds of pounding footsteps and paws above.

CHAPTER 3

*A*fter finishing her morning shift at the boutique, Sarah was up in the apartment, pacing in the living room. She pulled her phone from her pocket for the umpteenth time and let out a sigh when she saw she had no texts, messages, or missed calls. Of course, she wouldn't have missed any activity on her phone—she had the volume all the way up. But still, Adam hadn't gotten back to her, and it was starting to worry her.

Misty swept past her legs, then jetted toward the window. She glanced at the cat, then strode over to her, petting her soft fur.

"I wish I could be as carefree as you," she said to Misty, who simply meowed in response.

Sarah let out a long breath. She needed to get ahold

of herself. There were certain things she couldn't control, and it was clear she couldn't control the actions of others. If Adam didn't want to talk about what was going on, then she'd just have to get over it. She'd have to work hard to keep her emotions in check and squelch her burning desire to get to the bottom of things. What if there simply wasn't anything to get to the bottom of?

A spot of red out in the street caught her eye.

She squinted, getting a better look through the glare on the window.

Words slid from her mouth: "Well, I'll be…"

There, out toward where Henry Fudderman's bakery was, Sarah saw a man crossing the road. Sarah couldn't believe it—the man was wearing a red baseball cap and a black hoodie, despite the heat. Could it be the same man as last night?

There was only one way to find out.

Rushing away from the window, Sarah raced to the door, hurried down the steps into the boutique, and ignored Emma's calls as she rushed out the front door.

"Sarah?" came Emma's voice again, along with the jingle of the bell above the door.

Outside, the hot air took her breath away, and she gasped. Whipping her head to the right, she spotted the red hat among a sea of earth tones.

She crossed the street and kept her gaze fixed on the

man, who she hoped wouldn't see her following him.

The man was now past Fudderman's bakery, and he glanced over his shoulder once Sarah had crossed the street. She tried to keep her pace brisk, but didn't flat-out sprint after the man—that, she figured, would be too suspicious of her.

Speed-walking, she saw the man make a quick left down an alleyway between two brick buildings. Had he seen her? And if so, would he make the connection that she was the woman he'd been staring at the previous night?

Sarah broke into a jog, now that the man couldn't see her in hot pursuit, and she found the spot he'd slunk into.

At the end of the alleyway, she saw the man walking briskly at the opposite end, his red hat bobbing up and down as he went. Then, as quickly as she'd spotted him, she lost sight of him as he hung a quick right onto the street that ran parallel to the main strip.

Sarah launched herself along the alleyway, approaching a dumpster off to her left. Reaching the middle of the alley, Sarah caught motion off to her right, and before she could react, she slammed into a man who held a large bag of garbage.

The bag flung out of the man's hands and he gave her a scornful look, before quickly correcting his demeanor. "Sorry, ma'am," the man said, still slightly off-balance.

Sarah put an arm out and steadied herself against the brick exterior of the building. "No, it's my bad. I should watch where I'm going."

"Are you okay?"

Panting, Sarah nodded.

The man smiled as he picked up the bag of trash, launching it into the open dumpster. He tipped his head at her. "Good. Have a wonderful day."

"You too," she said and watched the man return to the building from which he came.

Sarah crept toward the end of the alleyway, where the mysterious man in the black hoodie and red baseball cap had just been. She was certain he was long gone, but she needed to be sure.

Once there, she looked both ways down the street that ran parallel to the main strip her grandpa's boutique was on. In either direction, among the dozens of people strolling about, she didn't see the bright red of the man's hat, nor anyone in a hoodie. People were going in and out of the shops on this street, having a wonderful time, but Sarah was stewing. She had to find this man—something about him was off, and she knew he held answers to what had happened the previous night at the amusement park.

Later that day, Sarah was in the kitchen with Grandma, baking. She was trying to get her mind off of everything that had happened, and one way was to focus on something else, such as creating culinary delights. Lately, she had been spending a lot of time with her grandma, learning all her secrets on how to bake the perfect cakes, brownies, and cookies. Today, they were working on a mango-lime cheesecake with a graham cracker crust. From reading over the recipe, she salivated at the thought of the cheesecake infused with mango and lime, and topped with a tart mango-citrus glaze and whipped cream.

Continuing her work zesting and juicing the limes, Grandma let out a long breath. Sarah glanced over at her globetrotting grandmother, seeing that she was fashionable, as always, in a light-pink blouse and slacks, though she was protecting her attire with a floral-print apron.

"I can't believe I'll be going back to work soon," Grandma said.

"Another cruise so soon? How long?"

Grandma nodded. "Another week-long jaunt. But I love it, sweetie. I spend most of my time baking in paradise, so what's not to love?"

Sarah smiled. To her, Cascade Cove was paradise, but she could understand how one could get so used to a place that another region was now considered a paradise.

"I've never been to the Bahamas," Sarah said, grabbing one of the limes to juice.

"Oh, it's lovely, dear. I'll have to take you on a cruise when I'm not working one."

Grandma got busy blending cream cheese with her electric mixer, then added sugar, eggs, sour cream, and vanilla. She then grabbed the mango-and-lime puree and lime zest and added those as well, until all of the ingredients were smooth and properly mixed.

"So, Grandma...do you use these recipes on the job?"

Grandma shifted her gaze to Sarah, ignoring her batter. "Yes, but not all of them because I'm busy working on extravagant cakes."

"Like what?"

"Oh, like five-layer cakes with fondant and decorations."

Sarah heard a pattering of footsteps behind her—Larry, with Rugby, Winston, and Misty trailing behind. The kitchen was a gathering ground for humans, canines, and felines alike—it was where all the culinary magic happened.

Larry's eyes grew wide as he approached a bowl of cheesecake batter. Without hesitation, he plunged his pointer finger into it, and Grandma was quick to swat his hand. "None of that, Lawrence!"

Larry didn't reply. Instead, he stuck his batter-covered index finger into his mouth, grinning with delight. "Mmm, I'm sure going to miss your baking, Ruth. Are you going to leave brownies in the freezer for me again? I'll be building that float all week for the Cascade Summer Parade and will be working up an appetite."

"No," Grandma said plainly.

Larry frowned.

Grandma continued, "Sarah is going to bake for you. I taught her how to bake the perfect brownie this week."

Sarah eyed her grandpa quizzically. "You're building a float?"

Larry beamed. "Sure am!"

"He does it every summer," Grandma said. "Oh, yeah, that's right—you're usually back in New York by now. Lucky you...you'll get to see the parade this year."

"So, Grandpa, what are you planning to build as a float?"

Larry's eyes shifted from the cheesecake batter to

Sarah. "I drew up a few sketches but haven't decided on one yet. And I'm glad to hear about those 'perfect brownies'—I'll need them to keep me going. I hope you bake them with the perfect crunch on the outside but chewy and soft on the inside, like your grandma does."

"And don't forget 'chocolatey,'" Sarah added.

"Oh, yeah, those nicely melted chocolate chips inside." Larry licked his lips.

Grandma and Sarah filled the kitchen with their chuckles.

At that, Larry left the kitchen, now satisfied that he had been able to taste the batter and that he'd have a supply of sweets to fuel his parade-inspired adventures. Winston and Rugby stopped by their bowls to lap up water, while Misty rushed off in another direction, likely to find a spot in which to nap the afternoon away.

"So, Grandma, when are you leaving for work?" Sarah asked.

"In a couple of days."

More footsteps trotted into the kitchen, and Sarah assumed her grandpa was back for a second helping of cheesecake batter, but when she turned to look, she saw Emma strolling in. Her cousin made a beeline for the fruit bowl, grabbing an apple. Tossing it in the air, she caught it and took a big bite out of the side of it. She leaned up against the door frame, savoring the fruit, and asked, "What are we baking today?"

"Mango-lime cheesecake," Sarah and her grandma said in unison.

Emma took another bite of her apple. "Sounds yummy. Mangos are my favorite fruit, well, besides apples."

Grandma glanced at Emma. "You know, I'd be happy to teach you."

"That's okay, Grandma. I already know how to bake. The amazing cookies I make are enough to satisfy my sweet tooth."

Exchanging a glance, Sarah and Grandma both grimaced. Sarah reflected on how her cousin's cookies were more like hockey pucks, and she never understood how her cousin could eat them. But Emma ate them all the time—by herself. Sarah figured her cousin would get the hint…

"So, Grandma," Emma said. "Have you heard anything about the person who died at the amusement park after we left the other night?"

Grandma shrugged. "I asked a few of my lady friends and some of the folks around town, and no one seems to know anything. One person said they heard it was a heart attack or stroke. Who knows?"

Sarah was beginning to pour the batter into the

prepared crust, when Emma asked her, "Have you heard anything from Adam yet?"

Sarah shook her head. "Not yet."

Keeping her eyes focused on her task at hand, Sarah felt her heart rate increase ever so slightly and she tried to focus her attention on baking, rather than the unsavory thoughts that took up residence in the recesses of her mind.

"Hmm." Emma took another bite of her apple. "So, nobody knows anything? That's weird. This is Cascade Cove, after all—Gossip Town, U.S.A."

"Oh, gosh," Grandma said.

Sarah glanced to her grandmother, who was hunched over at the open refrigerator. "What?"

"I'm out of whipping cream!"

"We can do this without whipping cream, can't we?"

Grandma spun around, a shocked look on her face. "We can't have a mango-lime cheesecake without whipped cream, dear. That would be a disaster."

"I'll go out and get some," Sarah said, finishing what she was doing.

"Are you sure?"

Sarah nodded. "I'll run over to the grocery store real quick, no worries."

"Oh, gosh, thank you," Grandma said, smiling. It was

clear she was relieved that the cheesecake wouldn't be a "disaster" without some whipped cream.

"Happy to help," Sarah said, then dashed out of the kitchen to save the day. If she couldn't figure out who the man in the red hat was, at least she could solve the only other problem at hand: a lack of heavy whipping cream.

CHAPTER 4

*S*arah pulled into the parking lot of the grocery store out on the western side of town. Finding a spot was difficult, but she pulled into an empty one near the back of the lot and killed the engine. She'd had barely enough time to run the air conditioner, so when she stepped out into the heat, her body didn't need quite as long to get acclimated.

Walking to the front of the store, she heard the sound of shopping-cart wheels against asphalt, seeing families with bagged food items. Many tourists ate all of their meals out, but there were some that stayed in Cascade Cove for several weeks, and eating out each and every day made for an exorbitantly priced vacation. Of course, many of the people she saw were locals, and she waved at a few as she strode toward the automatic sliding doors.

Inside, the grocery store was frigid, and she wondered if she should have brought a sweater. She chuckled at the thought as she strode along, dodging people with carts. One woman practically ran into her, too busy chatting on her cell phone.

Off in the candy aisle, a young boy was tugging at his mother's shirt. "Please, please, please..." the boy begged.

"That stuff will rot your teeth, Charlie," the mother replied.

Sarah said "hello" to them as she passed by, still hearing the boy's pleading until he was out of earshot.

At the back of the store, where the milk and cream were stocked, Sarah surveyed the selection, finding the spot where the heavy whipping cream was.

She pulled open the cooler, grabbed a carton of whipping cream, and then, through the glass of the cooler door, spotted a gentleman standing a few yards down. Her mouth dropped slightly when she saw his one discerning feature: the red hat adorning his head.

"There he is," she muttered, racking her brain to figure out what to say to the man.

When she closed the door, she eyed the man, but quickly noticed his gray hair. No, it wasn't the same man that she'd seen at the amusement park. It had been a coincidence, unfortunately.

The old man glanced at her, seeming a bit perturbed that she'd been looking at him for such a long moment, and in the next second, he lumbered away from her.

Holding the carton of whipping cream, Sarah figured the most logical next step was simply paying for the item and returning to her grandma. She'd have to search around town for the man she sought, but now wasn't the time.

Heavy footsteps behind her caused her to glance over her shoulder. A young man was opening a cooler door to grab a carton of milk, and she nearly dropped her whipping cream when she zeroed in on him. His black hoodie, disheveled from wear, was tight against his body, and his pale face was partly covered by the dark brown locks of hair that flowed from the bright-red baseball cap that sat atop his head.

He turned to look at her, slight surprise registering in his eyes.

"Excuse me," Sarah said, and the man quickly turned around, ignoring her as he walked away. "Excuse me," she repeated, but the man continued his march along the back of the store, away from her, then he made a quick turn into the cereal aisle.

Gripping the carton of whipping cream, she

marched down the aisle, watching the man grab a box from the shelf and then hurry along. Was he actually ignoring her, or had he not heard her?

"Hello?" Sarah called, hastening her pace.

Then the man whipped around, the strings of his hoodie flinging upward. "What do you want?"

"I saw you at the amusement park last night," she said, unsure of what else to say. She didn't want to throw accusations at a man she had never met, but she could tell something was bothering him, and that something could have been him having some information about the death or, perhaps, being responsible for it. She knew him still being at the scene might cause most to assume innocence, but in her mind, it might be unwise for a killer to *not* linger and mix in with the crowd.

"And I saw you," the man said. "You were staring at me and creeping me out."

"Uh, *you* were staring at *me*, and fidgeting, and—"

"Is it a crime to look at someone?"

"Well, no, but—"

"Have a nice day," he said, then turned around to walk away.

"Wait," she called after him. "Do you know what happened to the person who died last night? The accident."

The man turned around again, his face turning a

slight shade of red. He chuckled, though not out of amusement, then said, "So, you believe those lies, too? Is everyone in this town deaf?"

"Deaf...what do you mean?"

"Nobody heard the gunshot," the man said. "I even told the police about it, but for whatever reason, everyone still thinks it was an accident."

"Gunshot?"

"Yeah, a person was murdered last night."

Sarah's eyes grew wide, though for what reason, she didn't know. This only confirmed what she felt in her gut was true—that there was more to this than met the eye. What she couldn't understand was how this man was the only person to have heard the gunshot.

The man continued, "Shot and killed, and the police are keeping it under wraps."

"Are you sure you heard—"

"I was near the Ferris wheel when it happened." The man let out a sharp breath. "And nobody believes me when I say, someone *was murdered* behind the Ferris wheel."

"I believe you."

The man nodded, lips pursed.

Sarah continued, "Did you see anyone that night, anyone who—"

"I already talked to the cops; I'm not about to go

through another interrogation." The man turned around to walk away, then over his shoulder said, "I wouldn't go shouting around town that you know it was a murder... after all, the killer *is* still on the loose."

And with those final words, the man in the black hoodie and red baseball cap hurried along toward the front of the store, and in moments, was out of sight.

CHAPTER 5

*A*fter finishing baking with her Grandma, Sarah was out walking Winston and Rugby. The large, yellow lab was clearly becoming a handful for her grandpa, so she'd promised to walk him more often to wear off the "pent-up energy." Winston was happily along for the extra exercise as well, certainly not minding the warm, salty air, and all the sights and sounds of Cascade Cove.

Before leaving the apartment, Sarah had attempted to talk to Emma about what she had found out at the grocery store, but her cousin was too busy helping Larry with an errand. So, Sarah had decided it was best to walk along the boardwalk to see if she could find Adam, who was still ignoring her texts and calls.

Sarah strode along the boardwalk with the pups and

quickly regretted the decision—they were stopping to greet dogs and their owners every fifty yards. What good would this walk do Rugby if they were stopping so often?

Still, Sarah was happy to chitchat with other residents, as well as some of the tourists who were in town for a week or two. All of them lamented the "accident," but she didn't dare expose what she had found out. Of course, she knew, the man could have told her a lie. She hadn't heard anything about a gunshot ringing out. This man couldn't have been the only one to hear it, could he?

Sarah waved at Yuki Fujimoto as she passed by the Board Wok, the only sushi bar in town. Continuing along, Rugby and Winston seemed to be conspiring to force her to go faster, and for now, she was happy with the pace. At least they weren't stopping every few yards.

Then, the dogs' plan was foiled when Sarah spotted Adam off to her right. He was focused on jotting something down in his tiny notebook, and she wondered if it had something to do with the death at the amusement park.

"There he is," she said, steering the two dogs toward Adam, who was running a free hand through his short, dark hair. "Sorry, Rugby," Sarah muttered as they closed in on him, "looks like we're taking another break."

Sarah called out to Adam, who spun around in surprise and tossed his pen up in the air. It skittered on the ground, and he scrambled to pick it up. Standing up, he quickly realized it was her, and a genuine smile cast upon his face.

"Hey, Sarah. You scared me half to death."

"Speaking of, what happened the other night?" she asked, brows furrowed. "You left Teek's Tiki Bar abruptly after that phone call. Then I left you a couple of voicemails, texted you, and I don't hear a single peep from you. What's going on?"

"Nothing, it's fine." His tone certainly wasn't convincing.

Sarah placed her hands on her hips and tilted her head. "You're lying."

"I'm not lying." Adam glanced away, jaw set tight.

"Adam, you can't even look at me. Before you left, you told me someone died. Said you hoped it wasn't another murder."

At the word "murder," Adam focused his gaze on Sarah, keeping his eyes riveted to her.

"So, it is another murder, isn't it?" she asked.

Adam nodded.

Sarah leaned closer, hoping her lack of surprise didn't make him think she'd already been searching for answers elsewhere. "What happened, exactly?"

He glanced around a moment, then shifted his gaze back to Sarah. "Okay, fine. I'll tell you, but not here. We have to go somewhere private."

Adam motioned for her to follow him, and they strode along the boardwalk, toward a section that was much less busy. Rugby seemed happy they were walking again, but was soon disappointed when they found a secluded spot between two large sand dunes. Rugby whimpered softly, resigned to laying down in the only shady spot he could find. Winston sidled up next to him, giving him a nudge— he was in play mode, but Rugby wasn't having it.

"So," Sarah started, "how do you know for sure it was a murder?"

"I know because the victim was shot. And it's clear it wasn't self-inflicted."

Sarah nodded, showing no surprise.

Adam let out a sharp breath. "You already know about it?"

"Yeah. Some guy in a black hoodie and red baseball cap told me that someone was shot. Murdered."

"Todd Jenkins?"

Sarah shrugged. "I didn't get his name."

"I remember questioning him. He's the only one who claimed to have actually heard the gunshot."

"But how is that possible?"

FEAR AT THE FERRIS WHEEL

"We suspect it was during the fireworks show."

Sarah could almost kick herself for not thinking of it sooner. Of course, they were having fireworks that night. She just hadn't heard them from all the noise at Teek's. "Makes sense. So, was Todd the one who found the body?"

"No. An employee went back behind the Ferris wheel, where no one is allowed to enter, and right next to the platform, he found the body."

She pursed her lips, eyes cast downward. "So, that's three murders in one summer at Cascade Cove." Sarah furrowed her brows, meeting Adam's eyes. "No plans to make this public yet?"

"No. The amusement park attendant contacted his boss and the manager called us. We are trying our best to keep it quiet, as you know."

Sarah understood the logic and knew all too well that, until the killer was apprehended, the authorities liked to keep things under wraps, as to not disrupt the tourists and the businesses who depended on them visiting Cascade Cove. The last thing the small beachside town needed was public panic about a killer on the loose. Of course, people like Todd Jenkins didn't see things that way.

Adam continued, "Most people think it was just

someone who had a heart attack on the Ferris wheel. And we want to keep it that way."

"Who was the victim? And any leads yet?"

"No, and I don't want you to get involved."

"What? What is that supposed to mean?

"Exactly what I said. I don't want you involved at all in this. It's sort of why I wasn't calling you back—I know you'd ask me a million questions. And I should have never asked you to help last time. You almost got yourself killed, Sarah."

"I did not."

Adam gave her a look.

Sarah huffed. "Okay, I *could have* been killed, but I didn't *almost* get killed. There's a big difference."

"I never asked you to go after that person."

Sarah put her hands on her hips. "No, you didn't, and I don't need permission to do something, Adam."

"When it's police business, you do. It's dangerous, and things could have gone horribly wrong."

Before Sarah could reply, Adam's walkie-talkie squawked, a voice piercing through the static.

Adam pressed the "Talk" button and said, "I'll be right there."

"I gotta go," he said to Sarah. "We'll talk about this later."

Sarah stood there, dumbfounded, as Adam spun on

his heel and rushed away. For one, she hadn't been able to remind him that, since she was less intimidating than a police officer, she was able to wring information out of people, many of whom she'd known since she was a young girl. She'd helped him solve two crimes before, and to her, it felt like he was being too protective.

She gritted her teeth and made a mental note that she'd need to finish this conversation—she had a lot on her mind she needed to get out.

CHAPTER 6

ater that day, back at her grandparent's apartment above the boutique, Sarah rested in her grandpa's cushy chair, knitting needles in hand. Nearby, Rugby was snoring, his body twitching intermittently, as if he were chasing a squirrel in his dreams. Winston was also sleeping, though his snoring was barely audible. Misty was busy batting a toy around on the floor, while Emma laid on the couch, mystery novel in hand.

Clanging pots from the kitchen told her that Larry was at it again, cooking up something that was beginning to smell delicious. To her knowledge, he was making shrimp scampi with angel hair pasta, and normally she'd be chomping at the bit to dig into a meal like that, but her mind was still sour.

Sarah's brows were furrowed, and had been for several minutes now. She was down, and she had been since she and Adam had gotten into their "argument." She figured Adam probably considered it much less than an argument, but to Sarah, she was seriously peeved that he had denied her the opportunity to help. She was more than capable.

"What's the matter?" Emma asked, placing her book on her chest as she peered over at Sarah.

"Nothing."

"I know something is up; what is it?"

"What makes you think something is up?"

"You've been sitting there with your knitting needles, but they haven't been moving. You haven't made a single stitch."

Sarah gazed down at the puppy sweater in her lap. "Maybe I'm counting the stitches."

Emma cocked her head. "For twenty minutes?"

"Okay, okay." Sarah laid the needles and the sweater she'd been working on down on the table next to her. "I ran into Adam today."

Emma placed her novel on the coffee table, looking intently at Sarah. "Go on."

"I asked Adam about what happened at the amusement park the other night, and he said that a person was found shot behind the Ferris wheel. Then he tells me that he doesn't want me involved in the case, and we got into an argument." Sarah looked to the floor. "This is the first fight we've had."

"So, someone was found murdered behind the Ferris wheel? Do they have any leads yet?"

"Adam didn't tell me anything. And I didn't get much info from the guy in the red hat, either."

"You found him?"

Sarah nodded. "Learned about the murder from him. Apparently, he was the only person who heard the gunshot. Adam confirmed that bit of info. But I still can't believe he won't let me help."

Emma rose from the couch and approached Sarah, placing a hand on her shoulder. "Listen, Sarah, he's just worried about you. He wants to protect you."

Grandma walked into the living room and glanced at them. "You girls okay?"

"Yes, Grandma," Sarah said.

Grandma pointed to the kitchen with her thumb. "Dinner's ready, you know?"

A sudden crash came from the kitchen and ended with a rattling tray wobbling on the linoleum. A moment later, Larry's voice carried through the apartment: "Rugby!"

Grandma's eyes went wide. "What in the world?" She spun around and rushed into the kitchen.

Sarah glanced to the spot where Rugby had been sleeping and noticed he was gone. "Oh, no."

Sarah hurried into the kitchen, with Emma hot on her tail. There, in the middle of the floor, she spotted the rolls that were scattered everywhere. Rugby was busy gobbling them up while Larry attempted to push the lab away, but Rugby was winning this battle.

Face red, Sarah shouted, "Rugby! Leave it!"

Immediately, Rugby's ears dropped to flank his head and his tail jutted between his legs. Now sullen, he scampered back to his sleeping spot, defeated.

"I'm so sorry, Grandpa," Sarah said, and she and Emma helped him pick up what was left of the rolls off the floor.

"You need to figure out something with that dog," Larry said. "He's becoming a terror that I can't control."

"I'm not sure what's going on with him. I mean, I'm taking him for walks."

"Maybe he needs more."

"Maybe. Listen, Grandpa, I'll get him out more for exercise and will even start running him. Besides, I've been gaining weight and need to run it off, too."

Larry chuckled. "Must be your grandma's baking."

"And Henry Fudderman's donuts," Sarah added. She chuckled softly when she noticed Larry was wearing his favorite apron, which read, "Too Hot to Handel," with a picture of the famed composer. If she remembered correctly, Emma had bought that for him a few years ago as a birthday present.

Grandma stepped over to one of the cupboards and pulled out four plates, bringing them back to the table.

"Oh, Grandma," Sarah said, "let me help you with that."

"Thanks, dear."

Sarah helped distribute the plates in front of the four chairs that surrounded the table. Then she retrieved four sets of silverware and napkins and set the table, adjusting them slightly on the spotless, white tablecloth. Emma helped Grandma get the unsoiled food placed on the table as Larry grabbed a bottle of Dunham Vineyard's finest pinot grigio.

"Who wants some wine?" Larry asked.

Everyone said "me" in unison, and Larry poured each of them a generous portion.

Steam wafted from the large bowl in the center of the table, and Sarah smiled, as they all took turns fixing their own plates.

"This smells amazing, Grandpa," Sarah said.

Larry placed a napkin on his lap and grinned, taking an initial sip of his wine. "Dig in."

Sarah speared a piece of shrimp with her fork, then

twirled it to gather up some of the angel hair pasta. Taking a bite, she glanced at her grandpa, who winked at her.

"I take it you like my cooking now," Larry said.

"Uh-huh," she muttered, still savoring the buttery garlic scampi sauce. "I've always liked your cooking." Then she took a sip of wine, noting how its dryness contrasted the tender shrimp nicely.

Larry speared one of his own pieces of shrimp, getting some of the pasta on his fork, when Rugby raced by, knocking into his chair. The fork flung from his hand and the piece of shrimp skittered across the white tablecloth. Larry pivoted on his chair and eyed the dog. "Rugby!"

"Sorry, Grandpa," Sarah said as Rugby trotted off, toward where a rawhide lay. He grabbed the bone and started chewing, now too occupied to have a care in the world.

"It's okay," Larry said, but Sarah knew it wasn't. Between the torn-out underwear, the scattered dinner rolls, and now knocking into her grandpa while he was eating, Rugby was clearly acting out. He'd always been well-trained and well-behaved—these incidents were out of character for him. But Sarah knew it wasn't the yellow lab's fault—it was hers. She knew she needed to do better—to exercise him more and spend more time with him.

"I'll clean up the stain," Sarah said, starting to rise from her chair.

"Don't worry about it," Grandma said. "Enjoy your meal."

Sarah eased herself back down, feeling the flush in her cheeks.

"So, how was your day, you two?" Grandma asked, eyes shifting between Sarah and Emma. She was clearly trying to get the focus off of what had just happened.

"Sarah and Adam were talking about the murder," Emma blurted.

Sarah shot her cousin a look. "Emma!"

Larry regarded Sarah. "Another murder?" His face was awash with surprise.

Sarah clasped her fork. "Yeah, unfortunately."

"This is usually such a boring place," Grandma said. "Now, all of a sudden, there are people getting taken out left and right."

"Crazy, is what it is," Larry said to his wife. Then he turned back to Sarah. "So, what happened? What did Adam tell you?"

Sarah told them everything she had learned from Adam, every last detail about the person who'd been shot, which wasn't much. She realized she didn't even know the gender of the victim, let alone their name. Adam had kept virtually everything under wraps, and she realized she hadn't learned much about the victim from the man in the red hat—he was too quick to end their exchange in the grocery store.

Grandma cleared her throat. "The Cove's grapevine must be avoiding you, dear," she said. "I heard from one of my lady friends that the person who died was a man. Still young, maybe sixty or so."

Emma was sipping on her water and nearly spat it out. "That's young?"

"Sure is. I'd do anything to be sixty again."

"What else did your friend say?" Sarah asked.

"Hmm," Grandma said, chewing a piece of shrimp. She swallowed, then glanced at Sarah. "The man had three daughters and was an artist. He was a kind man who created beautiful beachside paintings for the world to enjoy."

"Do you know his name?"

Grandma's face scrunched up as she tried to recall the victim's name. "Um," she started, then a flash of realization swept across her face. "Abraham Dalton. People just called him Abe."

Larry gave his wife an odd look. "*The* Abe Dalton?"

"Indeed, Lawrence. The real-life art hero."

"Gee, Grandpa," Emma said. "I didn't know you were an art aficionado."

Larry chuckled. "You know, I do dabble in fine arts—just wait till you see the float I'm designing."

Emma rolled her eyes and Sarah followed suit.

Larry continued, "But there is a reason I know the name. There was a scandal a few years ago, if I recall correctly. Something involving Abe."

Grandma batted her hand at him. "Rumors, Lawrence. Nothing but speculation and rumors."

"It was in the newspaper."

"Bah, you can't believe everything you read in the paper," Grandma said, then she turned to Sarah, the corners of her mouth ticking up. "Listen, dear, you should go deliver the Dalton sisters some brownies. I'll make them tomorrow morning. You know where they live, right?"

Sarah nodded. "I think I remember—you point out their huge house every time we drive past it. Don't you want to come with?"

"I wish I could; I have to get ready for work, but please give them my condolences. I feel so bad for them —their mother passed a few years ago, and now they lost their father…"

Sarah took her fork and pierced another piece of shrimp, her mind spinning. On one hand, Adam forbade

FEAR AT THE FERRIS WHEEL

her sleuthing; on the other, this delivery would provide her the perfect excuse to ask the victim's daughters a question or two.

A simple question couldn't possibly hurt, could it?

Sarah knew there was only one way to find out.

CHAPTER 7

The next day, Sarah drove to the northern part of town, to where the Dalton sisters lived. In the passenger seat of her Corolla sat a large container of brownies, freshly made this morning by her grandma.

Having finally learned the identity of the victim, Sarah was eager to meet his daughters. What sort of information could she find out? She was anxious to know.

Once parked, Sarah carried the brownies toward the house and marveled at its architecture. The place was enormous and vintage, with several gables and a steep roof that came to a point. If the sun wasn't shining brightly in the sky, Sarah would have been unnerved by the structure, as it would have seemed better-fitted in a horror movie. She could practically see the bats sweeping across the pointed roof amidst the lightning bolts streaking the sky in her mind's eye.

Sarah rang the doorbell and waited.

An eerie silence.

Then she rang it again, shifting her weight as the seconds crept by. The door opened a crack, startling her, and she spotted a woman with jet-black hair and ghostly white skin peering out. The woman was thin, especially in the waist, and tall, but the detail that stood out to Sarah the most was the scowl adorning her face. Looking Sarah up and down, the woman didn't utter a single word. Perhaps she was waiting for Sarah to explain who she was, but Sarah couldn't be sure. All she knew was that the woman was slightly intimidating, with her piercing eyes boring straight through Sarah.

Sarah cleared her throat. "Um. Hi. I, uh, I'm Sarah. Sarah Shores. I have brownies." Sarah couldn't believe how ridiculous she sounded, so she simply held up the Tupperware container of brownies and waited for the woman to reply.

The woman's expression didn't change in the slightest—the scowl remained.

Just when Sarah thought she was about to die from embarrassment, a sweet and enthusiastic voice called from inside the house.

"Fern, who's at the door?" the voice asked.

Fern broke her eye contact with Sarah and inched away from the door as another woman approached. The woman was a little more hefty around the middle, but in a cute, jolly way, and her face wore a slight smile accented by a twinkle in her eye. She appeared to be in her thirties, yet she was dressed like she was decades older, wearing a flower-print dress.

"Good afternoon," the woman said.

Sarah felt only warmth from this woman, and her smile was contagious, a far cry from the vibe Sarah had gotten from her sister.

"Hi, my name is Sarah Shores—I'm Ruth Shores's granddaughter. She wanted me to come over and send her condolences." Sarah held up the brownies. "And I brought a batch of her brownies—she baked them this morning."

"Oh, how sweet of her. Do come in. My name is Rose, by the way."

Sarah stepped into the house, noting the same vintage look on the inside as she'd seen on the outside. There was a lot of dark wood with carvings and Italian doors leading from the massive dining area to the living room.

Rose turned to Sarah. "Please, feel free to have a seat in the living room. I'll take the brownies into the kitchen to serve them." Turning toward the living room area, Rose called out, "Lily, we have company."

A third woman approached the Italian doors that lead into the living room, holding a small pillow that was half-finished with flower patterns—apparently, she'd been busy with needlework. The woman, Lily, looked so much like her sister, Rose. Both women had light-brown hair in a curly updo, flower-print dresses, and were slightly chubby, especially around the middle, and both had round faces. They could've been twins, and they appeared to be about the same age. Even their personalities were similar. But, Sarah noted, they were very different from their sister, Fern. Sarah glanced back at Fern, noting the differences: she was taller than her sisters, and her sharp chin made her face look longer than theirs—not to mention those piercing, dark eyes.

Fern disappeared into the shadows of the hallway and Sarah suppressed a shudder. She followed Lily into the living room. The decor of the room, including the sofas, runners, and curtains, were either lace doilies or flower print. The doilies were placed on the end tables and the arms of the sofas for decoration, with pinks and blues being the most prominent colors.

Lily's soothing voice came out softly: "So, you say you're Mrs. Shores granddaughter?"

"Yeah."

"She's a lovely lady." Lily motioned to a couch. "Have a seat, and don't mind all the flowers. This is my parents' house, and my mother was a florist. She loved flowers so much that she decorated the entire house in flower print."

"Wow, she must have really loved flowers." Sarah knew that was an understatement, considering both sisters' names—Rose and Lily. She noted that Fern's name contrasted theirs.

"Yeah," Lily said. "Rose and I love them, too, so it all works out. Rose loves to host, and I enjoy being immersed in my needle work." She held her half-finished pillow up. "It helps keep my mind busy and off what happened to my father."

"I'm so sorry."

Lily nodded somberly. "Thanks. He was a sweet man; very quiet and kept to himself. I don't understand who would do this to him. He was loved my many people."

Out of the corner of her eye, Sarah caught a glimpse of Fern in the hallway, before she disappeared once again. She couldn't help but wonder why the woman hadn't said a word, and seemed to instead be monitoring them and what they were discussing. Something was quite off about the woman, and Sarah couldn't tell if she was still in shock over what had happened to her father, or if there was something deeper—more sinister —going on.

Rose entered the living room holding the brownies, which were now laid out on an elegant serving tray. "It's true," she said. "Everyone loved him."

Sarah regarded Rose. "I heard he was a painter."

"He was. That was his life. Would you like to see his studio?"

Lily smiled. "Yes, let's show her Daddy's studio."

Sarah returned Lily's smile. "Of course, I'd love to see it."

Rose set the brownies on a coffee table near the couch Sarah was seated on, and said, "Follow me."

Sarah rose from the couch and followed the women through the house, seeing old family photos on the wall. She couldn't quite make out who the people were, but she saw a younger Rose, Lily, and Fern in many of the pictures. Some were black and white, and she assumed they were of a young Mr. and Mrs. Dalton. She wanted to ask what had happened to their mother, but she didn't want to bring it up, with the recent death of their father.

Rounding a corner, Sarah followed the two sisters into an artist's studio. It was a large room with several easels and an ample amount of paint. Sarah noted the containers of paint thinners and how the room lacked windows.

"What about the fumes from the paint thinner?" Sarah asked.

"Our father had a vent system installed," Lily said. "He liked to be in complete solitude."

Sarah studied some of the paintings scattered on the floor, and a lone painting that rested on one of the easels. They were beautiful paintings, with a lot of cool blues of ocean water and warm tones of the sand and people enjoying the sun, relaxing or standing by the ocean and looking over the water. Sarah smiled, taking in the beauty of the artwork.

"They are quite lovely," Sarah said, still gawking at the paintings.

"Thanks," Rose said. "We love them. But we're not sure what we are going to do with this messy room."

"Probably leave it as it is," Lily added.

Rose nodded.

After Sarah viewed the paintings, the sisters led her out and back to the living room, where they ate brownies and chatted.

"I still can't get over how beautiful his artwork is," Sarah said, nibbling on a brownie.

"He was quite talented," Rose said.

"He must have had plenty of admirers."

Both sisters nodded somberly, letting the silence linger.

"Except that one time," Lily said, "with the hate mail—"

"So, Sarah, are you enjoying the brownies?" Rose said.

"Delicious," Sarah said, noting the redirect. She'd have to figure out what hate mail Lily was referring to, but now wasn't the time—she figured Rose would shut down any questions immediately. And besides, she had some other digging to do regarding their silent sister.

"How is Fern...taking things?" Sarah asked.

"Poor thing hasn't left the house since," Lily said. "She hardly goes out as it is, and is usually quiet, but after getting back from the amusement park the night it happened, well..."

"You know, Sarah," Rose said, picking up right where her sister left off, "you are welcome anytime for tea and biscuits."

"Thank you," Sarah said, smiling at the two sisters. She grabbed one final brownie and took a bite, glancing over to the spot where she'd witnessed Fern disappear into the shadows like a phantom. She couldn't help but wonder where Fern was now—what was the woman up to? Sarah couldn't put a finger on it, but there was something about Fern that just didn't sit right with her, and she couldn't shake the feeling that the woman's behavior was rather suspicious. And then there was the fact that Rose was redirecting every time Lily spoke frankly about the hate mail or the bit of information about Fern being at the amusement park the night of the murder. That would be a clear opportunity, but what could her motive have been? And who was the hate mail from, and did it have any connection to what had happened to Abe?

Sarah's stomach turned as those questions circled her mind, but she chalked it up to having one too many brownies.

CHAPTER 8

*A*fter her visit with the Dalton sisters, Sarah returned to the boutique, all the questions still swirling in her mind. The bell jingled above her head as she entered the shop, and she let out a long breath, relieved to be back.

Emma rose from her chair behind the counter. "Back already?"

"Emma, you won't believe what—"

Suddenly, Teek burst out of Larry's office, shirtless and holding a wrench. Sarah stopped short, surprised to see him.

An old friend of Sarah's, Teek was a great guy who always knew how to have a good time. In fact, when she was younger, he'd taught her how to surf and introduced her to his surfer lingo, not to mention encouraging her to get her belly button pierced. That last bit almost made her mom pass out when she saw the glistening stud on her daughter's navel. And her dad had remained speechless for weeks, a feat not many could accomplish.

"Teek, what are you doing here?" Sarah asked.

Teek smiled when he saw her. "Hey, Sarah. I'm helping your grandfather build his float."

"Aren't you usually surfing at this time of the day?"

"The beach is too crowded—too many goobers. Tourist season, you know how it is."

Sarah recalled that "goobers" meant annoying people, but she knew he wasn't speaking of the tourists in general, just those who thought they knew how to surf and were crowding the waters.

Larry strolled in from outside and zeroed in on the surfer dude. "There you are, Teek. I need that wrench." Then Larry noticed Sarah. "Hey, you're home. Good! Could you take Rugby out for some exercise? Maybe run him around until he conks out."

Sarah glanced at Emma, hoping to get her attention, but she was focused on their grandpa. Sarah really needed to talk to her, but what she wanted to discuss had to be done so in privacy. Turning back to Larry, she said, "Sure, Grandpa."

Larry motioned to the door. "He's on a lead out front with us."

Sarah scrunched her eyebrows. "How did I miss you guys out there?"

"We're working down the road a bit—couldn't find parking right in front of the shop. You must've come from the other direction."

"Ah, okay. So, has Rugby been any trouble?"

Teek smiled. "Nah, he's a good doggy."

"Yeah," Larry said. "Rugby seems to be good with Teek. He listens to him just fine. I just don't understand that dog." Larry shook his head. "Anyway, back to work, Teek. And don't forget the wrench." Larry spun around and headed for the door.

"Well, I guess that's my cue," Teek said and turned to follow Larry. Then he came to a stop, glancing over his shoulder. "Sarah, you should stop by at the bar. Haven't seen you in a while, dudette."

"It's only been a couple days, *dude.* Plus, I've been busy."

"Busy with what?"

"Just work stuff," Sarah lied.

"Oh, well, I have a Sandy Wave cocktail waiting for you when you have time." Teek gave a wink.

"Teek, you know I can't drink that stuff."

"That's okay. I invented a bangin' new drink—I call it the 'Sweaty Shell.'"

Nearby, Emma stifled a laugh.

"That sounds horrible," Sarah said. "You know, you can't just use an alliteration to name your drinks. They have to at least sound appetizing."

Emma chimed in: "What, like 'Fuzzy Navel' or 'Sex on the Beach'?"

Sarah sighed. "You know what I mean."

Larry poked his head in the door. "Hey, Teek! The wrench!"

Teek smiled at Sarah. "Gotta go!"

Emma shook her head, staring at Teek's glistening muscles as he exited the boutique. "He's quite a guy."

"Emma!"

"What? I'm allowed to look."

"How are you and Mark doing?" Sarah asked, trying to redirect. Mark, a local delivery man, was smitten with Emma, and always tried to pop in to see her while on his route.

"He's good," Emma said.

"So, Emma...I have to talk to you about the Dalton sisters."

"Oh, yeah? How are they?"

"They are, well...they're grieving. They just lost their

father, so that's expected. Nothing out of the ordinary there. Well, except..."

Emma took a step closer. "Except what?"

"One of the sisters seems a bit weird."

"How so?"

"I don't know. I think it's just her aura."

Emma straightened herself, furrowing her eyebrows. "What do you mean?"

"She's really quiet and...standoffish."

"What did she say?"

"That's the thing. She didn't say anything. Not one word." She wished she was exaggerating, but she wasn't.

"Are you sure she's not a mute?"

It was Sarah's turn to furrow her brows. "Maybe she is, but I doubt that's the case. Anyway, one of the sisters let it slip that Fern hadn't been out of the house since the night of the murder. And you'll never guess where she was."

"Where?"

"The amusement park."

Emma's eyes got wide. "Well, isn't that something. So, she was there? You don't think she was the one to pull the trigger, do you?"

"I don't know. I can't figure out *why* she would off her father. What could her motive possibly be?"

"Who knows. I guess we'll have to do some digging."

Sarah nodded. "Just seems like she's got something to hide. Skeletons in the closet. And then, I forgot to mention, Lily slipped, saying something about hate mail."

Emma placed her hands on the counter, leaning against it. "What hate mail?"

"No clue. She just mentioned it, then Rose cut her off."

"Strange. Maybe you should call Adam and see what he thinks of all this."

"He doesn't want me involved, remember?"

Emma leaned closer. "He just cares, and he got worried about you."

"I'm not calling him. Besides, he'll only say I'm speculating. He won't understand how odd Fern's behavior was."

"Yeah, it does sound weird, but it could just be how Fern is grieving. I doubt she'd kill her own father, anyway."

"Maybe you're right," Sarah said, nodding, though as the words rolled off her tongue, her mind still trying to come up with reasons why Fern would want her own father out of the picture.

CHAPTER 9

*L*ater that day, Emma and Sarah were in the boutique, helping customers. It felt like the day was going by at a snail's pace. Teek was still outside, helping Larry, and every once in a while, Sarah could hear one of them yell out in pain amidst the nearly constant banging of a hammer.

"What are they doing out there?" Emma asked.

"I don't know, but whatever it is, I'm sure it doesn't need that many nails!" Sarah moseyed over to the window to catch a glimpse of what they were constructing. "There's nothing even on the float yet!"

Sarah returned to the counter as the last customer left the shop. She let out a long breath—finally, a lull in customers.

"I was thinking about what Fern's motive could be," Sarah said. "And—"

"You still think it was her? Just because she was there, doesn't mean she did it. A lot of people go to the amusement park."

"Not this woman. They said she hardly ever leaves the house. So why would she go out that night? It's quite the coincidence."

"I can't believe I'm about to say this, but...you're *jumping to conclusions!*"

Sarah stood, hardly able to believe what her cousin had just said. Typically, Emma was the one who always jumped to conclusions, and Sarah had to continually squelch that urge. But now, the tables had turned. Still, Sarah had some thoughts on the matter she had to get out—

Just then, the bells jingled at the front door to the boutique. A tall, good-looking man in a brown uniform strolled in, whistling a happy tune.

"Hi, Emma," the man said, grinning.

Sarah let out a frustrated breath—hashing out ideas at work was an exercise in futility...

"Hey, Mark," Emma said. "What have you been up to on this hot and humid day?"

"Oh, you know, living the dream."

"Always good. Sporting the shorts, too, I see."

Emma glanced down, and Sarah followed her gaze. The man's legs were so white, they were blinding.

"Looks like you need a tan," Emma continued.

"I'm with Emma on that," Sarah said, making a show of shielding her eyes.

Mark shrugged. "I'm not a shorts kind of guy."

Emma stepped closer to the man. "You live in Cascade Cove! What do you mean, you're not a shorts kind of guy?"

"Guess I just don't like having my legs exposed. I usually wear pants, but it's just too hot today."

"Quite a sacrifice on a hot day," Emma said with a grin. "So, do you have a delivery for me?"

"Nope! Came here to ask you out."

"Again?"

"Yup. I know of a new seafood place that just opened up. It's called Ahoysters."

Emma tilted her head. "Ahoy-what?"

"Like, 'Ahoy, matey,'" Mark said in his best pirate voice, "but with oysters! Ahoysters."

Emma giggled. "You've got to be kidding me. That's the dumbest name I've ever heard."

"I think it's pretty awesome. So, you in?"

"I—"

"Great!"

Emma crossed her arms. "I didn't say 'yes.'"

Sarah knew Emma secretly wanted to, though. She seemed to really like Mark.

"Well, let me know, Emma. I gotta get going! The boss is watching."

"How?"

"GPS."

"On you?"

"No, on my truck. They know what stops I make and when. I had a delivery for Patricia a few doors down and walked over here, but they will probably catch on pretty quick if I don't get going soon." Mark started heading for the door. "You've got my number, Emma. Give me a ring if you want to go." He swiveled his head toward Sarah as he passed her. "Bye, Sarah!"

"So long, Mark! Enjoy the heat in your styling shorts."

"Always do!"

The bell jingled again as Mark headed out, and when Sarah was about to make another attempt at hashing out her theories on Fern, Grandma came strolling into the shop through the door that led up to the apartment. She was wearing her two-inch heels, red lipstick, and form-fitting slacks with a white blouse and a blue scarf. Sarah noted the pair of sunglasses she wore and the rolling suitcase by her side. She almost looked like a movie star, ready for travel.

"Well, off I go," Grandma said. "Where's Lawrence? I have to leave soon, or I'll be late."

"Grandpa, Grandma's leaving now!" Emma shouted.

"Emma, dear, why don't you just walk out there and get your grandpa instead of shouting?"

"Sorry, Grandma. It's just easier."

Grandma frowned.

Emma hurried to the door, opening it slightly, and yelled out. Sarah could feel the hot and humid air rushing in along with Larry as he dusted off his hands.

"There you are, dear," Grandma said with a big smile. Sarah couldn't help but smile, too. Her grandparents were always affectionate and still smitten over each other, ever since they were young lovers. The black-and-white photos she'd seen still held a place in her mind—and in one of Grandma's scrapbooks. "How is the float coming along?" Grandma asked him.

"We're just building the platform today," Larry said.

"Have you decided on what you're going to have on the float?"

"Not quite. I had Teek look over my sketches of what we could build, and he says that they're good, but he has a better idea."

"What is it?"

"It's supposed to be a surprise! I think you're going to love it—I'll send you pictures!"

"As long as it's not like the Dalmatian you built that lifts its leg and pees on a tree."

Sarah stifled a laugh at the thought. Though she hadn't been around for the parade during what her Grandma had called the "Dalmatian Diuretic Disaster," she'd heard about it often enough and had seen pictures of it as well.

"Hey," Larry said, wiping sweat from his brow with a handkerchief, "that was a great idea, and people loved it. And it drove business, you know. Sales went up after that."

Emma shook her head and mouthed, "No, it didn't," to Sarah.

"Well, Lawrence," Grandma said, "I'm sure whatever you come up with will be just fine. As long as it's not a repeat of that year's parade..."

Grandma rushed over to her husband and gave him a giant hug and a big kiss, before she gave both Sarah and Emma a hug in turn. "Stay out of trouble, girls."

Emma smirked. "Don't we always?"

The door swung open and Teek entered the boutique. "Leaving already, Mrs. Shores?"

"Yes, Teek. I'll be back soon."

Teek strolled over and gave Grandma a bear hug, lifting her off her feet. It was quite the sight to see a muscular surfer dude hugging a five-foot-two, petite older woman.

"Oh," Grandma said, as he engulfed her.

He put her down gently. "Have a good trip, Mrs. Shores."

Grandma adjusted her clothing and fixed her hair. "Why, thank you, Teek." She grabbed the handle of her suitcase and rolled it along with her as she moseyed to the front door.

Sarah and the rest of them said their goodbyes to Grandma as she strolled out the door to where her pink Cadillac was parked. She was off to work, but in truth, Sarah knew it was another adventure her grandma couldn't wait to embark upon. Hopefully, by the time she returned, things would be back to normal in Cascade Cove. Sarah could only hope the fact a murder had taken place would remain under wraps until the killer could be apprehended.

Sarah turned back to her cousin, glad to get a moment without distraction. "As I was saying, I was thinking about what Grandpa said about the 'scandal.'"

"You think there was a scandal that Fern was involved in?"

"I'm not sure. But it's worth investigating. Also, since Abe was a well-respected, 'big-shot' artist, I'd assume his paintings would go up in value upon him passing..."

"You think Fern killed her father so the paintings would go up in value and she could sell them? All behind her sisters' backs?"

"Maybe."

"What are you going to say next, that they're all in on it?"

"No, that's ridiculous. The sisters wouldn't have told me about Fern being at the amusement park if that were the case."

"Unless they were working together with Fern, but now are actively trying to push her under the bus."

"Hmm," Sarah said. "I hadn't thought of that. But they both seemed so nice."

Emma chuckled, plopping down on her stool. "Looks can be deceiving."

Sarah nodded. There was certainly a lot to mull over.

CHAPTER 10

*T*hat evening, Rugby and Winston were sleeping in the apartment, tired from the heat and their short jog with Sarah. Misty was cleaning herself in the middle of the floor. Any time the dogs were asleep, she took advantage of what was prime time for a cat like her to groom herself.

Sitting in her grandpa's comfy chair, Sarah heard him call from the kitchen, "Who wants to go out?"

Sarah turned to look at Larry, who was leaning back against the counter, exhausted from building the platform for the float. He'd already taken a shower and was now obviously starving.

"Sure," Sarah said. "What did you have in mind?"

"What about the Banana Hammock?"

"We go there all the time, Grandpa. Don't you want to try another place?"

"Wait, isn't there that new seafood place that just opened?" Larry asked.

"Ahoysters?" Emma said, coming out from one of the back rooms of the apartment.

Larry looked suddenly spry. "That's it! We should try that place. I love oysters, and I love pirates."

"Oh, I don't know if we should go there," Emma said, taking a seat on the couch.

Sarah grinned at her cousin. "Is it because Mark wants to take you there?"

"Be quiet, Sarah!"

"Who's Mark?" Larry asked, confused.

Sarah rose from her chair, her back cracking as she stretched. "You know Mark. The guy Emma's been dating."

Emma's eyes went wide. "Sarah!"

"What?"

"I'm so confused," Larry chimed in. "Are we going to this new place or what?"

Emma scoffed. "Fine, we'll go to Ahoysters."

After finishing getting ready to go out, Sarah, Emma, and Larry strode out toward the boardwalk and headed down to where the new restaurant was located. Sarah spotted the sign and chuckled at how the name was spelled: "Ahoy!sters."

"The exclamation mark really adds to it," Sarah said.

"Yeah, and you gotta love the giant pirate with the parrot on his shoulder." Emma pointed.

Larry grinned, opening the door for his granddaughters. "I already love this place."

Inside, they were greeted by a spunky young man in a pirate's outfit. "Ahoy! Would ye like a table for three?"

Larry nodded, a grin fixed on his face.

"Arrrr, follow me, mateys!"

Emma rolled her eyes, but Sarah knew her cousin was secretly loving every minute of this experience. Following the man, Sarah heard several dozen voices melding into one. She scanned the large room and saw the place was packed. On the walls were pictures of pirate ships, a few replica wooden steering wheels, and other memorabilia. To top it off, a wax figure of a pirate stood proud in the corner, holding a replica cutlass that glistened in the candlelight.

"Shiver me timbers, there is but one table left," the man said, motioning to a lone empty table. He set down three menus, all printed on old, brownish-colored paper that looked more like parchment than modern printer paper.

"Do you serve clams?" Larry asked, not bothering with the menu.

The man smiled and bellowed, "Yarr! We serve clams by the bucket!"

Larry's eyes grew wide. "By the bucket?!"

"Certainly, seadog! We also have fresh oysters, raw and nude, served with cocktail sauce, horseradish, lemon, and crackers."

Emma nudged Sarah. "'Seadog' means an old pirate —he just called Grandpa old."

"How do you know?"

Emma motioned to the cell phone she had clasped in her hand. "Internet."

Sarah glanced over at her grandpa. He was still deliberating over the clams and oysters.

"That's a toughie," Larry said.

The man nodded. "Ye best take yer time. Be back in a few, mateys."

Sarah let out a sigh. The pirate schtick was already getting old. She peered down at her menu, overwhelmed by the number of dishes that sounded incredible.

Scanning the page, she noticed the waiter had already come back.

"Have ye decided between the clams and the oysters, matey?" he asked Larry.

Larry shook his head.

The man in the pirate get-up continued, "If ye can't decide, we also have a Seafood Bouillabaisse. It includes the freshest lobster, shrimp, scallops, haddock, mussels, clams, and crab meat tossed in a light marinara sauce with shells."

"Oh, my," Larry said. "I'd like that, please."

"Aye! Blackbeard would be proud!" He turned to Emma. "And for ye?"

Emma glanced up from her menu. "Um, chicken skewer with rice and veggies."

Sarah glanced at her cousin in shock. "Aren't you going to get any seafood?"

Emma considered the question, then asked the man, "Do you have crab rangoons?"

"Sorry, ma'am, me don't have that."

Sarah shook her head. "This isn't the Board Wok," she muttered.

Emma furrowed her brows. "Hm. What about the lobster rolls? Can you make that a side?"

"Aye, me can." The man then turned to Sarah and asked, "And what would you like?"

The man was clearly getting worn out from saying "aye," "ye," and "matey," and had slipped with his dialect.

After sliding a finger down the menu to her selection, Sarah looked up at the man. "I'll have the Lobster Scampi with garlic, butter, and wine over angel hair pasta." Sure, she'd just had her grandpa's shrimp scampi the previous night, but she couldn't turn down the promise of fresh lobster.

The man nodded and gave one final, enthusiastic, "Yarr!" but Sarah could tell he was tired after working most of what was probably a long shift.

He strode away toward the kitchen, and moments later, Sarah spotted Henry Fudderman approaching them. The parts of his cheeks not covered by his white beard were rosy red as usual, reminding her of Kris Kringle. He was close to Larry's age, though instead of gray hair, he had a head of hair so white, it looked like a blanket of pristine snow.

"Larry!" Henry said, holding out both hands. His voice boomed, and a few people at a neighboring table glanced over, clearly perturbed. "How are you, my friend? And Sarah, Emma, you're looking well. Did you enjoy the Boardwalk Fudge Cake you got the other day?"

"Sure did," Sarah said, memories of the delicious Fudderman creation swirling through her mind.

"How do you like this place?" Larry said to Henry. "Pretty swell, isn't it?"

"It's my new favorite!" Henry scanned the table, then frowned. "Where's Ruth?"

"On another cruise."

"Ah! That's nice. So, have you heard?"

"Heard what?"

"Abe."

"The painter?"

"Yeah, it's such a shame," Henry said. "Here we are, all enjoying the fireworks, and that genius perishes on the Ferris wheel. Heart attack, if you can believe it."

Sarah bit her tongue, not wanting to let the truth be known about what had actually happened to Abe. Eyeing her grandpa, she was glad when he glanced back at her, understanding that what she'd told him about the murder wasn't public knowledge.

"Hard to believe," Larry said.

Sarah let out a long breath.

"Yeah, it was a strange night," Henry said.

Both Sarah and Emma perked up.

"You were there?" Sarah asked.

"Yeah, I never miss the fireworks. And I just so happened to be standing near the Ferris wheel—probably at the exact time poor Abe was...well, you know. I should have known something was going on..."

"Why's that?"

"Well, I saw a man running away from the Ferris wheel. Not just jogging, but flat-out sprinting. After I heard about what happened to Abe, I realized it was someone going to get help. I guess he wasn't fast enough."

"Are you sure it was a man?"

"Yeah, sure as can be."

"Do you remember anything about the man?" Sarah asked.

"Why?"

"Just wondering."

Henry scrunched his eyebrows down, deep in thought. "Hmm, well, I do remember he was wearing a uniform."

"Like the employees at the amusement park always wear?"

"Yeah. He must have been the ride operator. Not sure why he didn't just use his walkie-talkie. All the employees there are always on those things. I figure it was because of all the noise, with the fireworks."

"Anything else about him you remember?"

"Um, yeah…for some reason, I recall him having red hair, freckles, and he wore glasses. He was young, but not a kid."

"Henry, dear…your food is getting cold!" came a woman's voice from behind Henry.

Henry whipped his head around. "Thanks, honey. Be right there." Turning back toward Sarah and her family, he said with a smile, "I'll see you around. Take care, everyone."

Stepping away from the table, Henry left just as the man in the pirate outfit was bringing their food order. Sarah spotted the steam wafting from the delicious-looking entrees. But her mind wasn't focused on how yummy the food was. Instead, she was focused on figuring out who this red-haired, freckled, bespectacled amusement park employee was, and why they were running from the Ferris wheel at the same time Abe Dalton was being murdered. Another suspect had just been added to her list...

Tonight, she'd have to take a trip to the amusement park.

CHAPTER 11

*L*ater that night, Sarah and Emma strolled south along the boardwalk, toward the amusement park. Off in the distance, Sarah spotted the Ferris wheel. Not long ago, a man had been shot and killed there, and just the thought of it made her uneasy. Now, she was going to figure out who exactly operated the Ferris wheel and why they had been running from it during the fireworks show, at the time the victim was said to have been killed.

Inside the park, Sarah led Emma toward the bumper cars, which were a stone's throw away from the giant wheel. She motioned over to where the Ferris wheel operator stood, squinting to see. "I don't think that's the right guy. He doesn't have red hair or glasses."

Emma crossed her arms. "Should've brought binoculars."

"Then we'd give ourselves away, Emma." Sarah peered around, then strolled up to the bumper car operator, a middle-aged man who was as thin as a rail. He wore the same uniform as all of the other ride operators: khaki pants with a tucked-in blue polo.

"Excuse me, sir," Sarah started.

"Get in line," the man said, pointing. His voice was stern, a testament to how seriously he took his job—or perhaps it had been a long shift.

"No, I'm not here to ride," Sarah continued, "I just have a question."

The man ignored Sarah, instead staring at the riders in the bumper cars with a frown fixed to his face. There, on the ride, two young teenaged boys were laughing as they tried to punch one another whenever their cars passed by each other. The man turned on his microphone and muttered, "All hands and feet must stay in the cars at all times. I repeat, all hands and feet must stay in the cars at all times." His voice echoed, almost unrecognizable over the loudspeaker.

The man turned back to Sarah, a long breath escaping his gaping mouth. "What's your question?" he asked, monotone.

"Do you know someone with red hair, freckles, and glasses who works here?"

While Sarah waited for a reply, she glanced to her right and noticed that the two teenaged boys were still goofing off and laughing. But, at least, they weren't trying to hit each other with their fists anymore. Just their cars.

The ride attendant ignored the sound of bumper cars crashing behind him and said flatly, "Hmm, yeah. That sounds like Pete Melinsky. I haven't seen him since that night the ambulance was here. I guess some guy had a heart attack or something on the Ferris wheel. Pete hasn't worked since."

"He hasn't? Why?"

The man shrugged. "Maybe the incident was too much for him. I don't know. I heard the guy might've died. But they've been tight lipped around here about it."

"Do you know anything about Pete?"

"Not really. He's quiet—keeps to himself."

One of the teenaged boys on the ride had somehow shimmied out from the bar that was meant to hold him inside the car and was practically standing as he attempted to smack his friend. Someone bumped him from behind and he almost spilled out of the car.

Face flushed, the ride attendant swung around and slammed his open palm onto a red button nearby. The ride shut off immediately, and a dozen groans melded into one.

The man shook his head. "Teenagers—always ruining it for the rest of the kids, you know?"

"Yeah, gotta love them," Sarah said. "Well, anyway, thanks for your time."

The man ignored her words and got back on his microphone, as Sarah and Emma walked away from the bumper cars, hearing his garbled words echo over the speaker: "All hands and feet must stay in the cars at all times…"

Stepping farther away from the ride, Emma glanced at Sarah. "That's a bit suspicious. The guy hasn't come back to work since the murder."

"Yeah," Sarah said, "and he's quiet and keeps to himself—much like Fern…"

Turning to watch where she was walking, Sarah spotted Adam strolling toward them. He looked like he'd been working out lately—he'd probably taken Teek up on his offer to meet at the gym several times a week. She was glad they were both getting along. Sarah could tell his biceps and shoulders were already a bit larger, and it made quite a difference under his police uniform.

Adam smiled. "Hey, having fun tonight, Sarah?"

"Nothing like a night at the amusement park."

"It's pretty humid, if you ask me."

Sarah nodded. It was still hot, even after dark. All of Cascade Cove was waiting for a good rainstorm to cool things down, but they hadn't had such luck the past couple of days. "Yeah," she said, "well, even on a hot night, sometimes you just need to get out of the house."

"So, you know Will?" Adam asked.

"Will?"

Adam motioned to the ride operator Sarah and Emma had just been talking to. "The guy working the bumper cars."

"Oh, right! Will!" Sarah nodded. "Yeah, great guy."

"Kind of a miserable guy, if you ask me."

Sarah hesitated a moment, unsure if Adam was testing her. "Uh...yeah, he can be miserable."

Adam crossed his arms and furrowed his brows. "You wouldn't happen to be questioning him about what happened the other night—were you?"

Apparently, she'd failed his test, but she wasn't ready to give in. It was Sarah's turn to cross her arms. "I don't think that's any of your business. So, what are you doing here, anyway?"

"Security. I still work for the police department."

"But they have security here."

"I have to do my rounds, and you know that includes the amusement park. Sarah, I'm asking you to please not get involved in this. It could be dangerous. You don't have the training I have to handle these situations."

"I'm the one who solved the last two cases. If it wasn't for me, those horrible people would be running free."

"That's not true. We would have captured them eventually."

"Oh, 'eventually.' Well, I feel safer already."

"You have no idea—"

"I think I have some idea."

Adam huffed. "Sarah, why do you have to be so stubborn?"

"I don't know, Adam; why do you have to be so controlling?"

Emma butted in: "Guys, guys!" She stepped between them, where the tension was still as thick as the humidity. "It's hot and muggy, and it's making everyone miserable. And you two blowing more hot air around isn't going to help anyone." Turning to Sarah, Emma continued, "I think it's time we head home, anyway."

Sarah dropped her shoulders and nodded. Her cousin was right—arguing with Adam wasn't a good use of anyone's time, and certainly wasn't going to help anyone.

Emma then faced Adam. "Have a good night, Adam.

Stop by at the shop sometime. Grandma missed you today."

Adam nodded, his jaw still set tight. Sarah knew he was still stewing over what had just been said, though just like her, he was biting his tongue.

With her cousin leading the way back home, Sarah sidled up next to her. "Sorry about that, Emma. Sometimes he just...urg!"

"Yeah, I know. Passion can get so heated."

Sarah nudged her cousin. "That's not funny. I'm really mad at him."

"Hey, you don't have to tell me. I can sense it, and I understand. Besides, you two were a great distraction."

Sarah gave her cousin a confused look. "What do you mean?"

Emma held up her phone. "I got something you might be interested in!"

"What's that? Your phone?"

Emma turned her phone toward Sarah and said, "What's *on* my phone. Check this out—I took this picture."

Sarah squinted at the phone's screen. "Is that...an address?"

Emma nodded. "Pete Melinsky's address."

"How'd you...?"

"Like I said, Sarah, you two were a great distraction. I

think the park manager was afraid one of you were going to let what happened at the amusement park slip too loudly. He was outside watching, with his office door wide open behind him. And, lucky for us, he was so focused on your argument that he didn't notice me slip in behind him and pull up one of his employee's addresses on his computer. I think he was in the middle of payroll or something. I just had to scroll down to 'Melinsky' and—bingo! It was too easy!" Emma laughed mischievously.

"Emma! You could get in big trouble for this. What if they have cameras?"

Emma swatted the air. "If they had working cameras, we'd know who the murderer was already."

"True."

Emma waggled her eyebrows. "Well, I guess I know where we'll be going tomorrow."

Sarah nodded. "To find Pete Melinsky."

CHAPTER 12

The next morning, Sarah and Emma convinced Larry to take a break from constructing his float, to watch the boutique while they headed out for some important "errands." In truth, their errands were vitally important: the newest suspect in the Abe Dalton case had to be found, and fast.

Fortunately, through her cunning, Emma had procured the man's address. Sarah still thought Emma would end up being found out for the stunt she'd pulled in the amusement park manager's office, but perhaps it would be days before they'd review any surveillance tape, if one existed. As Emma had said, if they'd had functional cameras in the amusement park, the killer would have been apprehended by now.

But the killer was still on the loose, and Sarah knew

it was up to them to figure out the killer's identity. While Sarah still held her suspicions of Fern, the stand-offish ghost of a person who'd had opportunity and perhaps even a motive to kill her own father, Pete Melinsky had been seen running from the scene of the crime around the same time Abe had been shot. Perhaps he'd shot Abe dead and rushed to escape the scene. And the fact that he hadn't been to work since that fateful day seemed awfully suspicious and put him at the top of Sarah's suspect list.

In her Corolla, Sarah punched Pete's address into her GPS, realizing it was in the western section of town, out near the main grocery store. With Emma in the passenger seat, Sarah drove to their destination.

Less than a block from the address, Sarah spotted an apartment building—a two-story brick structure that was so mundane, she could hardly stand it. But, this was the place she was looking for, the place they were likely to find some answers.

She found a space in the small parking lot, and she and her cousin got out, striding confidently to unit number twelve. Steeling herself, Sarah rapped on the door and waited.

Silence.

She knocked again, this time louder.

More silence.

"I don't know, Sarah," Emma said. "I don't think he's home."

Sarah knocked a third time, louder yet. This time, a neighbor's door opened and another tenant, a burly man, came out and eyed Sarah and Emma.

The man practically bore a hole straight through them, and his biceps flexed. Sarah was about to turn and run before the man tossed them both up in the air and juggled them, but then he finally spoke, his voice nearly as high as hers: "What are you doing, causing such a ruckus out here? I'm trying to watch the latest episode of *Darkness Into Light*."

"Uh…isn't that a soap opera?" Sarah asked, holding back a chuckle.

"Sure is. Only the best show ever."

Sarah and Emma exchanged a quick glance, but both kept their composure. "Uh-huh," Sarah said. "Well, listen, we're looking for Pete. Have you seen him?"

"Nope. He hasn't been home for the last few days."

"Do you know where he is?"

The man nodded. "At his sister's. I think her name is Shelby."

Emma chimed in, "Oh, Shelby. Yes, I remember her. She's the tall, blonde girl who used to hang out with Teek back in the day. She was older, like, at least ten years older than him. That caused quite a stir in the town..."

"Great!" Sarah grabbed Emma's hand and hurried away, barely thanking the burly man in her haste.

"Sarah," Emma said, "where are we going?"

"To Shelby's, of course."

"You know where she lives?"

"No. Don't you?"

Emma shook her head, and they both stopped abruptly.

"I thought you knew her," Sarah said.

"I said she used to hang out with Teek."

Sarah sighed. "Maybe Teek knows where she lives."

"Yeah. Let's go talk to him."

They hurried to the Corolla and hopped in. Pulling out, they drove back toward the main strip, turned right, then followed the road up to find a parking spot not too far from Teek's place.

"Are you sure Teek will know Shelby's address?" Emma asked.

"I don't know," Sarah said absently. Her gaze drifted, and in her peripherals, she spotted a man rushing from the pharmacy, his red hair bright in the afternoon sun. She did a double take, seeing his glasses, and when she returned her gaze to the road, she had to slam on the breaks—a pedestrian was crossing the street.

"Watch out!" Emma shouted.

"I know, I know. Look—it's our friend, Pete."

Sarah waved at the pedestrian, who scowled at her. Then she pulled over, eyeing the man who hurried into his classic red Dodge Charger. His car was on the same side Sarah was now parked, and she waited for him to pull out, then eased out to follow him from several car-lengths behind as he jetted down the street. She pressed on the accelerator, knowing she had passed the posted speed limit.

To heck with it—this was worth the risk of getting pulled over. She couldn't let her top suspect get away. She had to figure out where he was going, and why he was in such a hurry.

After a ten-minute drive, following Pete's car way beyond the town's limits, Sarah spotted the bright-red car pull over. Sarah parked a hundred yards behind, and saw the man bolt from his car, running toward a house that sat on a large property.

"Think that's Shelby's place?" Emma asked.

"No idea."

Sarah studied the house. It was a lovely brick home

with white shutters. Small and simple, it had two miniature bushes on either side of the front door and a flamingo lawn ornament that added a welcome accent to the landscaping.

"Are we just going to sit here?" Emma asked. "I didn't think we would be on a stakeout."

Sarah unbuckled her seatbelt and her cousin followed suit. She got out of the car and made a straight shot to the walkway that led to the house. Hurrying along, she ascended three steps to the stoop, with her cousin by her side.

Sarah was about to ring the doorbell, when Emma whispered, "What will we say to him?"

"What do you mean?"

"Well, we can't just show up and say, 'Hey, someone saw you run from a crime scene a few nights ago, and we'd like to know if you murdered a man.' Maybe we should pretend we're from the Census Bureau."

Sarah rolled her eyes. "Just follow my lead." She pressed the doorbell and waited.

Moments later, the door opened, exposing a man of medium height and build. Sarah saw his glasses, mop of red hair, and face littered with freckles. They'd found Pete Melinsky.

Sarah cleared her throat. "Hi, my name is Sarah Shores, and this is Emma."

Pete nodded. "Hi, there. Can I help you with something?"

"Yeah, do you happen to know Ruth Shores?"

Pete scratched his chin. "No, I don't believe so."

Sarah glanced at Emma, who raised one eyebrow at her. Sara returned her gaze to Pete. "How about Abe Dalton?"

"Uh, yeah, isn't that the guy that had a heart attack or something at the amusement park a few nights ago?"

"Yeah."

"How is he?"

"He's dead," Sarah said bluntly.

Pete's eyes grew wide. "Oh, no! How terrible. What happened?"

"Well, it seems that someone might have murdered him."

"What?"

Sarah could tell by the man's reaction that he was genuinely surprised, but she still spoke the words that were on her mind: "Someone saw you run from the Ferris wheel during the fireworks show."

Pete's eyes narrowed. "Well, I *am* one of the ride operators of the Ferris wheel. Now, if you'll excuse me, I—"

"Abe was murdered during the fireworks show. Was

shot right behind the ride you operate. The ride you were running from."

A few beads of sweat sprung up on his brow. With clenched fists held by his side, his voice was firm: "Listen, I don't know who you are, but you should go bother someone else. I'm busy."

Before Sarah could get a word in edgewise, the man slammed the door in her face.

"I guess we *should* have pretended we were from the Census Bureau," Emma muttered.

Sarah glanced at her cousin. "He's still awfully suspicious, don't you think?"

CHAPTER 13

The following day, Sarah was in the kitchen, baking one of her grandma's cakes. With the cake already in the oven, she was left with the task of making the frosting. She began slicing fresh strawberries to put in the frosting like Grandma had told her, brows furrowed as she worked.

"Something's not quite right with Pete...What am I missing?" she asked the empty kitchen as she sliced the final strawberry.

The oven bell dinged, and she grabbed a pair of mitts, opening the oven to see that her cake was over cooked and burnt around the edges.

Sarah grimaced, knowing the cake would be dry.

She put on the pair of mitts and pulled the cake out, setting it down on top of the oven. Taking off the mitts, she pressed a finger to the cake, but in her daze, her finger touched the corner of the pan, searing her skin.

"Ow," she shrieked, yanking her finger away. She stuck her finger in her mouth as she rushed to the sink to pour cool water over her burn. Her day couldn't get any worse.

As she was holding her burnt appendage under the cool tap water, she heard a bouncing noise off to her right.

It was Emma, bouncing a small, red ball on the kitchen's linoleum floor. Her cousin moseyed over to the cake and inspected it.

"Hm, I don't know, Sarah. I could be wrong, but I don't think there is supposed to be a well in the middle of the cake."

"What?" Sarah looked at it, shaking her head.

"Looks like someone punched it in the middle," Emma said, pointing and snickering.

"Ha-ha, laugh it up."

"I'm just kidding, Sarah."

Sarah turned back toward the sink to tend to her wound, and Emma asked, "Are you okay?"

"I'm fine—I just burned myself."

"No, I mean..." Emma inched closer to Sarah, catching her cousin's eyes. "Are *you* okay? Like, *mentally* okay."

Sarah sighed. "I'm just trying to wrap my head around what happened with Pete."

"We ticked him off, that's what happened."

"But if he didn't kill Abe, why didn't he just tell us that?"

Emma shrugged. "I don't know. I guess that's what we need to figure out."

"It just doesn't make sense—what motive would he have?"

"Beats me."

"I just can't help but wonder, what does some dude like Pete, a ride operator at the amusement park, have to do with a local artist? I hate to typecast someone, but he seems more like a guy who spends his time working out and cruising around in his muscle car than the type who is into art. Now, Fern, on the other hand..."

Emma cocked her head. "You still think Fern would have something to do with her own father's death? What could her motive possibly be?"

"She's more likely than Pete, I think."

"How?"

"Like Pete, she has opportunity, but I think she has more to gain from his death. Like we were talking about before, his paintings' values would probably go up, and maybe the sisters are hurting for money."

"They live in a huge house, don't they?"

"Yeah, but it was their parents' place. Their mother is gone, and now their father, but maybe they are struggling. They do share a single car between the three of them. Maybe their taxes are high…I don't know."

"But that doesn't mean she murdered him," Emma said.

"Well, we'd need to find proof of motive."

Much to Sarah's chagrin, Emma began bouncing the ball on the floor again, and said, "I still don't think it's Fern. Now, Pete, he's as suspicious as they come. And, of course, don't forget—"

Suddenly, a flash of bluish fur streaked across the kitchen floor and swiped the ball as it bounced back up. Pouncing up and snagging the ball midair, the fur-ball took off out of the kitchen and down the hall. Sarah could hear the jingling of the tiny bells attached to Misty's collar as she escaped the scene. Sarah and Emma followed quickly behind the feline, and found Misty on top of Grandma's bookshelf, her tail dusting the binds of her scrapbooks.

"Misty, where's my ball?" Emma asked.

The cat meowed and leapt off the bookshelf, causing one of the scrapbooks to tumble and land with a thud on the floor. Sarah cocked her head—the scrapbook had landed open on the floor.

"Ugh," Emma said, stepping away from the book and

in the direction Misty scurried. "She must have hidden the ball in her secret hiding spot, under the corner table." Emma strode toward the table.

Eyeing the scrapbook, Sarah bent down to retrieve it, and one of the pictures on the open page caught her attention. On the right of the page was a picture of a woman with red-rimmed glasses, holding a year-old baby on her lap. The baby was smiling and had cute, blonde, curly hair. The headline read, "Cascade Cove's Donna Covell: Secrets to Balancing Work and Motherhood."

Sarah scanned the page and noticed a picture on the left, showing the same woman with light hair and her signature red-rimmed glasses. She wore a bright smile that contrasted with her all-black attire, which was accented by a large, decorative scarf. Behind her were several canvases of art.

Sarah's eyes narrowed. "Oh my." Studying the picture, one of the art pieces made Sarah pause. It looked awfully familiar.

"Hey, Emma! Come here."

Turning, Sarah spotted Emma on her hands and knees under the table, undoubtedly searching for the red ball.

Glancing back at the scrapbook, Sarah read aloud to herself: "Donna Covell's new art gallery is now open...

displaying local artists."

She whipped her head toward Emma again. "Emma, come look at this," Sarah said, voice loud.

Emma grunted, and Sarah could still hear the tiny, jingling bells under the table. "Gotcha!" Emma said proudly, and Misty scurried out from under the table and back up onto her spot on a top shelf.

Seconds later, a thump sound. "Ow!" Emma crawled out from under the table, rubbing her head. She walked over to Sarah, ball in hand, yet it didn't seem like it had been worth the effort.

"What is it, Sarah?"

"Look." Sarah pointed at the picture. "This woman owns an art gallery here in Cascade Cove. Behind her are paintings by Abe Dalton."

Emma leaned in, taking a closer look. "Yeah, maybe she knows something."

"That's what I was thinking. Maybe she knows something about that scandal Grandpa saw in the paper...Or perhaps she knows the Dalton sisters and can shed some light on them." Sarah returned the book to the shelf and hurried into the bedroom she and her cousin shared, pulling on her sneakers. She glanced back at Emma. "Are you coming, Emma?"

"Can't. Got a date with Mark."

"Ooooh," Sarah said. "Who am I to stand in the way

of romance? Besides, it might be best if I do this one solo."

"Okay, sounds good. While you do that, I'll do some snooping online to see what I can dig up about Pete Melinsky."

"Thanks, Emma. I'll see you later, then."

Sarah raced past her cousin, on a mission to get some answers about the Dalton sisters. Only time would tell if talking to Donna would produce any meaningful clues or shed light on the motive of Abe's killer.

CHAPTER 14

Sarah eyed the building that housed Donna's art gallery. The outside looked a bit dingy and small, and so far, unimpressive. Sarah wondered how in the world this place was an art gallery, and hoped that looks were deceiving.

Strolling to the door, Sarah entered the building and her eyes went wide. Like Teek's Tiki Bar, the outside had apparently been a facade. The brightly lit room was spacious and there were large, framed art pieces of contemporary still life, portraits, and abstracts of various mediums that lined the white walls. In the middle of the room sat a desk, and standing behind it was a charming lady with red-rimmed glasses. Her dirty-blonde hair was shoulder length and swept across the gray and dark-blue shawl that wrapped around her neck, accenting her all-dark attire. She looked older than in the picture Sarah had seen, but Sarah knew for sure it was Donna.

Sarah approached the desk, still scanning the room and gawking at the artwork.

The lady smiled. "Hi, can I help you?"

"Yes," Sarah said, "I was wondering if you carry any pieces by Abe Dalton."

The lady shook her head. "No. I'm sorry, but we haven't sold any originals from that artist since 1986."

"That's okay, I'm not exactly looking for originals."

The woman adjusted her glasses. "Prints? I do have a series Abe was working on for years."

Sarah nodded.

"Give me a moment, ma'am, and I'll see what I have." Donna walked into a back room of the art gallery.

While the woman was busy looking for the prints, Sarah glanced down at the desk and noticed a framed picture of Donna with another, younger woman. The woman had shoulder-length blonde hair, much like Donna, and a smile that could light up a room. Her royal-yellow blazer contrasted her black blouse beneath, and the stunning jewelry around her neck spoke volumes about her classy tastes.

Clicking heels could be heard from the back room, and moments later, Donna returned with a portfolio, setting it on the desk.

Donna spotted Sarah eyeing the picture and smiled. "That's my daughter, Claire."

Sarah's gaze shifted upward. "She looks just like you."

"I get that a lot. She's a good girl—knows her art and is very independent."

Sarah smiled back at the woman.

Donna placed both hands on the portfolio, smoothing it. "So, here are the Abe Dalton prints." She opened the portfolio and pointed to the first print. "These are the beach series he had released in the eighties. He did a painting of Cascade Cove's beachside, one for every month of the year. He said that he wanted to capture the beach's natural beauty here in our hometown every month."

Sarah flipped through the prints. She noted his recognizable style, visible brush strokes with lots of color. The early months of the year featured vacant beaches, some with only a single person standing, looking out into the distance. As Sarah flipped through each month, getting into the summer months, she noticed that there were more people and crowds, with umbrellas and children building sandcastles.

"These are stunning," Sarah said. "Why don't you sell the originals?"

"I simply don't have them. Abe's always been very protective of his artwork. He liked to hold on to his originals, even though they could sell for thousands. But he only sold prints here."

"I see," Sarah said, flipping through the prints some more. Then she stopped, confusion sweeping across her face. "Uh, where's June's print?"

"I don't have it," Donna said. "Never did."

Sarah looked up, eyebrows furrowed. "What do you mean?"

Donna took a seat at the desk, crossing her legs. "Well, there are two theories. Either he never finished the series, or some say he did finish it, but he just never released the June print, for whatever reason. If that's the case, then the June painting would be worth a pretty penny. Someone could retire on what the original would fetch. Even a print could go for quite a bit." Donna raised her eyebrows.

"That's odd of him to skip the month of June, though, isn't it?"

"Well, he once told me that he didn't paint them in order. He liked to wait until he found inspiration. Said that if he didn't see or wasn't inspired by anything beautiful worth painting, he simply wouldn't paint anything. I guess we'll never know about June's painting."

"I guess not," Sarah said, flipping through the remaining prints.

"Though…" Donna started, then hesitated.

"What?"

"Oh, I was just thinking about his daughters. I'm sure they'd have all of his originals. Perhaps even the June painting."

"You think they would sell the paintings?"

Donna glanced down at the book of prints. "If they're anything like their father, they wouldn't, but who knows…" Locking eyes with Sarah, Donna said, "I heard they are having financial problems, even before their father's unfortunate death."

"How do you know that?"

"Oh, you know this town," Donna said, still smiling pleasantly. "The rumor mill spins faster than most of the rides at the amusement park."

Sarah's heart beat slightly faster. If what Donna said was true, and the paintings could allow one to retire off the sale proceeds, then the sisters had plenty of motive to murder their father. Perhaps her cousin's theory of Rose and Lily trying to push Fern under the bus was true. But why not go to the police in order to incriminate their sister?

Pondering over these questions, Sarah decided she needed to drop by and visit the Dalton sisters. She had a feeling she was getting closer to unmasking the killer, or killers, in this case. Only time would tell if that feeling was correct.

CHAPTER 15

*A*fter leaving the art gallery, Sarah headed straight toward the house that the Dalton sisters shared. Reflecting on the information gleaned from her visit with Donna, Sarah was sure that the sisters had quite the motive. The paintings could, in fact, pull them out of their current financial crisis, if what was circulating around Cascade Cove was true. She could practically hear the voices of Adam, Grandma, and even Emma in her mind. They would say it could be hearsay—nothing but speculation and rumors.

Sure, it could be hearsay. Perhaps the sisters weren't going through financial problems, though the high value of the paintings could induce greed in them—and greed was just as much of a strong motive as the fear of getting deeper into financial trouble.

Parking her car in front of their house, she felt her phone buzzing in her pocket. She pulled it out and saw that it was Adam calling her, but she slid it back into her pocket, letting the call go to voicemail. She would deal with him later—besides, she knew he was probably checking in to ensure she *wasn't* sleuthing. The last thing she needed was another reminder to leave things to the authorities, who were much too slow for her liking.

As Sarah approached the front door, she paused and whipped her head around. She could have sworn she'd seen motion out of the corner of her eye. A person?

Scanning around, she didn't see anyone.

Chalking it up to paranoia, Sarah continued toward the door and knocked confidently. A few moments later, the door opened, and Sarah saw Lily standing there, welcoming smile fixed to her face.

"Sarah! Do come in," Lily said. "We're about to have biscuits and tea."

Sarah entered the house and took a deep breath, taking in the aroma of freshly brewed tea as she sat down in the dining area. Rose stepped over, holding a cup of tea served in a fine piece of china.

"Thank you," Sarah said. "What kind of tea is this?"

"Darjeeling black tea."

Sarah took a sip of the tea, enjoying the mild spiciness. She watched as Rose stepped away, but then the woman returned less than thirty seconds later with the biscuits, jam, and butter. "Here you are, Sarah. Enjoy."

The women joined Sarah at the table, and they chatted while sipping tea and nibbling on the biscuits. Sarah spread a small amount of butter on her biscuit, then added some strawberry jam, which she thought complemented the biscuits and black tea nicely.

"I still can't get over how amazing your father's artwork is," Sarah said. "It's stunning."

Rose took another sip of her tea. "Thanks."

"I heard he also painted a beach series, but I don't remember seeing it when you showed me his studio."

"Ah, yes," Lily said, nostalgia clearly getting the better of her. "That was a beautiful series he worked on for years."

Sarah glanced at Lily. "I heard it wasn't finished."

"Wasn't finished?" both sisters asked in unison.

"June's missing."

"Well," Rose said, "we don't know much about that."

"Yeah," Lily chimed in. "We assumed it was finished."

"Would you mind if I saw the originals?" Sarah asked.

Lily brought her napkin up to her mouth, giving each side of her lips a quick dab. She kept her gaze fixed on the cup she held. "We don't know what he ever did with the series. We just figured he sold them."

"Really? The lady at the art gallery says that he never

sold his originals there. Do you think he sold them privately?"

"Oh, you mean Donna? Isn't she a lovely lady?"

"Yes, she's very nice. So, do you know anything else about the originals? Where they might be?"

Rose set her cup down in its saucer and the resulting *clink* echoed through the room. "Oh, dear. I don't know where the originals would be for that series. He must've sold them through another curator. We never fussed with his art business, and he was never very vocal about it. A very quiet man."

Sarah tried to keep her face neutral. She recalled what Donna had said about Abe having always been very protective of his artwork, that he had liked to hold on to his originals. What Lily and Rose had just said contradicted what Sarah had learned from Donna. Perhaps the sisters weren't being truthful. Of course, that was assuming what Donna said held any truth to it.

Out of the corner of her eye, Sarah caught a glimpse of Fern in the dark hallway, looming ominously. In the next moment, when she and Fern locked eyes for an instant, she disappeared as if she'd been an apparition. Sarah leaned to her right, craning her neck to see further down the hall.

"Are you okay, dear?" Rose asked.

Sarah returned herself to her original sitting position. "Uh, yes. Thought I saw someone."

"Must've been Fern. She's really shy."

"Quiet, like Daddy," Lily said.

"Was your father a sociable man?"

"Not really. He kept to himself, focused mostly on his art."

"But he was well liked?"

"Oh, yeah. Everyone loved him."

"So, no enemies?"

Rose glanced up, locking eyes with Sarah. "Why do you ask?"

Sarah took her napkin from her lap and dabbed her mouth, trying to maintain proper etiquette. "I was just curious. I thought Lily had mentioned something about hate mail during my last visit."

Lily said, "Yeah, there was a man who—"

"Lily, there was no hate mail, remember?" Rose interrupted, shooting her sister a quick glance, then returned her gaze to Sarah. "Would you like more tea and biscuits, Sarah?" Rose asked.

Before Sarah could decline, Lily spoke up again: "Oh no, Rose. We are almost out of biscuits."

"Oh, dear. We'll have to get more on Wednesday." Rose turned to Sarah. "We do our shopping on Wednesdays."

"That's right," Lily said. "We haven't missed a Wednesday grocery shopping excursion in twenty-five years! And with only one car between all of us, it works out perfectly. Rose and I are homebodies, so Fern gets the car every day except Wednesday. Besides, Wednesdays are the least busy days at any store. That's why we picked it." Lily lowered her voice. "And this Wednesday is Fern's birthday—she'll be forty. We'll be getting her a carrot cake, her favorite."

Sarah smiled. So, at least one detail Donna had given Sarah checked out: the sisters shared a single car. And, she'd just learned a tidbit of information about Fern, and the fact that Wednesday might be a good time to get the mysterious woman alone. But she couldn't quite shake the second instance of Rose dodging the whole hate mail detail. She'd have to bring that up when she spoke with Fern. "Oh, her birthday's coming up?" Sarah asked. "That's nice. So, Fern goes out a lot?"

"Not really. Especially not since Daddy passed."

Sarah couldn't help but noticed Lily's use of the word "passed," as if she hadn't heard her own father had been murdered. Perhaps she was trying to make it seem as if she didn't know the truth. Or maybe she just wasn't one to use harsh words such as "died" or "murdered."

"So, Sarah," Rose said. "Did you want more tea? We

have plenty. And you could have the last of our biscuits, if you'd like."

Sarah glanced at Rose. "No, thank you," she said. "I'd better get going anyway—need to get back to the boutique. Thank you for the tea and biscuits. They were delicious."

Rose scooted her chair back. "I'll see you out."

Sarah waved the air. "No need; I can see myself out. Thank you." Though it was true that Sarah was more than capable to see herself out, she figured this was a good way to get away from the two sisters and maybe speak to Fern one-on-one before she left.

Rose shook her head. "No, Sarah. I insist. Besides, I like to lock the deadbolt."

Sarah couldn't argue with that, and walked out with Rose behind her. Once Sarah was outside, Rose said her final farewells and then shut and locked the door with an audible *click*.

Darn. If only she could get a moment with Fern, even for just a minute. Then, she'd be able to gauge her body language when asked direct questions about her father and the night of his unfortunate "passing." She hoped to also glean some information about the location of his original paintings. And then there was the hate mail, which Rose had just denied. Perhaps Fern could shed light on all of that.

Walking back to her car, the beginning of a plan to get Fern alone was forming in her mind. But she'd need Emma to hash out the details—and provide support for what she was brewing.

CHAPTER 16

*S*arah drove back to the boutique, tapping her fingers on the steering wheel as she went. She couldn't wait to talk to Emma, but then she realized that her cousin was out on a date with Mark. Hopefully, she'd be back soon—Sarah had a lot to go over with her.

Parking her car on the street, Sarah spotted Larry and Teek still working on the float. They had completed the platform, and a red board was nailed to it, but other than that, nothing else seemed to have been finished, and Sarah still had no idea what it was supposed to be.

Before Teek noticed she was there, she saw him with Rugby by his side. He muttered something to the yellow lab, and the dog obeyed his orders immediately.

"Good dog," Teek said, excited. Then he tapped a

hand lightly on the side of his thigh, and Rugby followed him as he walked around the float.

Teek spotted Sarah and waved. She strode over to them, and heard the loud bang of a hammer hitting wood, then Larry's cries.

"Son of a gun!"

"Larry, you gotta stop hitting the wrong nail, man," Teek said, shaking his head. Rugby barked once, as if he were giving his two cents on the matter.

Larry lumbered out from behind the float, and Sarah could see his cheeks were flushed. He had been working so hard, and she felt bad for him, though she was glad Teek was here to help out.

"Hey, Sarah," Larry said, wiping sweat from his brow with a hanky. "Where's your cousin?"

"Oh, Emma's out on a date with Mark. I think they went to Ahoysters."

Larry scratched his head. "Mark?"

"Grandpa, you know Mark."

"Oh, that's right," Larry said, a sudden flash of realization on his face. "The guy who brings us presents every day."

"Presents?" Teek asked. "Tell him to stop by my bar."

"He means deliveries. Mark is our deliveryman."

Teek chuckled. "You had me going, you kook," he said to Larry, who simply batted his words away.

"Well, have fun, you two," Sarah said. "And, Grandpa, watch out for your fingers, okay?"

"Okay."

"Hey, Sarah," Teek said. Rugby was sitting next to him, wagging his tail and looking proud. Teek patted him on the head, making his tail wag faster. "Check this out."

Teek took a step away from the yellow lab by his side. "Rugby!" He snapped his fingers, and Rugby quickly turned to face Teek. "Down boy!" Rugby laid down, obeying the order flawlessly. "Roll over!" Rugby rolled over, amazing Sarah even more. "Now give me some skin!" Teek put his palms out toward the lab, and Rugby jumped up like he was giving Teek a high five but with both paws

"Wow," Sarah said. "He doesn't even listen to me that good! How did you teach him so fast?"

Teek shrugged. "Dunno. I guess dogs just always liked me. Welp, back to work we go!"

"Have fun."

Sarah stepped away from them, and heard Teek give Rugby another command. Over her shoulder, she watched the dog follow his words to the letter. She had to wonder about her old friend—had he been a dog trainer at one point, or did he just happen to be good with animals?

Sarah approached the boutique's front entrance and noticed the sign on the door had been flipped to CLOSED. She pulled the door open and entered. Inside, all of the lights were out except for a few spotlights behind the counter. She let out a long breath, enjoying the silence that was broken only by the faint pattering of paws above her. Misty or Winston was milling about up in the apartment. Soon, she'd join them and relax.

She ascended the steps and moseyed into the apartment. Misty was up on the couch, where Emma usually sat to read her mystery novels. For a moment, Sarah felt like she was a character in some mystery book—the sleuth, perhaps. She wondered what her "character" self would do in the situation she found herself in.

Plopping down in her grandpa's chair, she ignored the knitting needles nearby, opting instead to close her eyes.

Her "character" self would probably be a bit more proactive. Sure, she'd stopped by to talk to Donna and had visited the sisters a second time, but she knew she had to figure out a way to get Fern alone. And she knew she needed to find out if the sisters had Abe's paintings somewhere or if he had actually sold them.

In Emma's mystery novels, Sarah knew the sleuth usually had some sort of sidekick, either human, feline, canine, or otherwise. Sarah knew Emma was more of a sidekick than anyone she knew. The yin to her yang. The Watson to her Sherlock. She couldn't wait to hash out the rest of her plan with Emma. And maybe Emma had found some juicy details about Pete Melinsky, the man Henry had seen running from the Ferris wheel at the time of Abe's murder. She couldn't shake how suspicious he'd been acting. Did he have anything to do with the esteemed artist's death?

As Sarah sat there, thinking, the minutes turned into hours, and when she looked out the window, she could see darkness descending upon Cascade Cove.

Outside, she could hear her grandpa still hammering, and envied him—he was in his own little world out there. Sarah, on the other hand, didn't have the blissful distraction of building a float for a parade during a time of crisis.

But then she remembered the one thing that now drove her crazy: mostly everyone, except a few people, understood Abe's death to have been the result of a heart attack. So nobody else was really working to solve this thing, except for Adam and his ilk, but Sarah knew that, though their hearts were in the right place and they were an honorable bunch, they were simply too slow for their own good.

Waiting for Emma to return home, Sarah picked up her knitting needles and got to work on another dog sweater. Her eyes grew heavy, and soon, she found herself lumbering back to the bedroom, plopping into bed. In less than two minutes, she was asleep.

CHAPTER 17

Sarah's eyes sprang open and she rolled over, swinging a hand to find the cell phone she'd left on the nightstand. Eyeing the screen, she shot up in bed.

It was ten o'clock in the morning—she couldn't believe how late she'd slept in!

Glancing over to her cousin's bed, she saw that it was already made. Then she realized that Emma hadn't even gotten in by the time she'd fallen asleep.

She got dressed and hurried into the bathroom to get ready, assuming that Emma would be somewhere in the apartment. But she was nowhere to be found.

"Hmm," Sarah muttered, "I wonder where she is..."

Not even bothering to get a bite to eat, Sarah

descended the steps into the boutique. There, behind the counter, sat a tired-looking Emma.

"So…" Sarah started.

Emma glanced at Sarah, then turned back to her computer, tapping away on the keyboard.

Sarah inched closer to her cousin. "How was your date?"

"Good."

"Just good?" Sarah asked, plopping down beside her. "I need more than 'good.'"

"We went to Ahoysters."

"And?"

"The pirate guy outed me!"

"Outed you?"

"Yeah. He said, 'Welcome back, matey,' and then Mark gave me a look. I thought he was mad that I went there without him after he'd asked me to go, but instead he asked me what dishes were good."

"He's so nice," Sarah said, realizing how true her statement was. Mark was a perfect fit for Emma. He was nice, handsome, and able to not only take Emma's sarcasm, but one-up her every time. Sarah cleared her throat—she had other things on her mind.

"Oh, so I did some digging on Pete Melinsky," Emma said.

Sarah leaned closer. "What did you find out?"

"Well, I mentioned it to Mark, and he said that Pete *was* there the night of Abe's death."

"How does Mark know that?"

"He saw him running, too, I guess. Anyway, Mark and Pete used to be close friends, and Mark said he called Pete up, asking if everything was okay. Turns out Pete was running away from his station that night because he received a phone call that his sister took a turn for the worse."

"Shelby?"

"Yeah, the doctors thought it could be pneumonia, so Pete left in a hurry to be there for her. Apparently, she's still struggling with her illness."

"Wow."

"Yeah, and it all checks out. I got in touch with a few people on social media, asking them about it, and they all say the same thing, that Shelby is sick and Pete has been taking care of her."

"That explains why we saw him leaving the pharmacy and going back to her place. He was probably picking up her meds."

"Right. So, what did you find out? You went to see that woman at the art place?"

"Yeah, I met Donna, the art gallery owner."

"And?"

"Well, I was able to see the prints, but she doesn't sell

any originals. In fact, she said that Abe is very protective of his work. I checked out the prints, and he had a beach-themed series—one for every month of the year—but June's print was missing."

"Hmm."

"Yeah. She said if the original June painting was ever sold, it would fetch a lot of money. And she did mention that the Dalton sisters were going through financial trouble—I mean, the sisters themselves even claimed to share a single car between the three of them."

Emma glanced up from her computer. "Interesting. What else?"

"After finishing up at Donna's, I stopped over at the Dalton sisters' place, and they made it seem like their father might've sold his paintings. And when I brought up the missing June painting, they seemed like they didn't know much about it."

"You think they're lying?"

"Someone is lying, either Donna or the sisters, but I don't know why Donna would lie about anything. Oh, another thing that was weird: when Lily referred to her father's murder, she used the word 'passed.'"

"That could be nothing."

"And then, there was the second mention of hate mail. Lily brought it up again. You should have seen

Rose's reaction to that. She said there was no hate mail, then she quickly diverted the conversation."

"Why would she cover up the fact that there had been hate mail?"

"I don't know. It could have something to do with that scandal Grandpa mentioned."

Sarah looked expectantly at her cousin, but Emma's gaze was fixed on her computer screen, in deep concentration.

"What are you doing?" Sarah asked.

"Checking online," Emma said. "Maybe I can find something that could shed some light on all of this."

Glancing over Emma's shoulder, Sarah saw her cousin was looking up Abe Dalton on social media.

"Here," Emma said. "We can see what kind of reviews he has since his social media page is set up as a business account." She scrolled down and came across a one-star review, then another. "Hmm…"

"Are those all from the same guy?" Sarah asked.

"Yeah, looks like he has reviewed Abe's work several times."

Sarah squinted. "What does it say?"

"Each review is super harsh, Sarah. Listen to this: 'Abe is a con artist, that much is clear. He sold me prints, claiming they were originals! I've been robbed, and I'm going to make sure he never does anything like this again!!!'"

"Wow," Sarah said. "That's crazy. I didn't know artists sold prints as originals. Is there a way to find out how to get a hold of the guy who left those reviews? We need to talk to him—he could be the same person who sent Abe that hate mail."

Emma glanced at Sarah. "Maybe you should tell Adam. I mean, this is quite a motive, if I ever saw one."

"I'm not telling Adam. No way. He'll know I'm going around talking to people—he'll put a stop to it, for sure. Listen, Emma. Please, just help me figure out where we can find the guy who left those reviews. Even if I call Adam, it'll probably be better if I talked to that man—I'm a little less intimidating than a man in a uniform with a badge."

"Okay, Sarah. Give me a second."

Furious tapping emanated from where Emma sat. Sarah couldn't believe how fast Emma was, like she was some kind of computer hacker, digging into government databases.

"Got it!" Emma said.

"Wow, that was quick."

"What can I say, I'm a computer hacker extraordinaire."

Sarah suppressed her laughter—she and her cousin thought so much alike. "So, what did you find?"

"Well, he listed his place of work on his profile: Hal's Paints."

"You're amazing, Emma."

Emma cracked her knuckles. "I know."

"Time to go shopping for art supplies," Sarah said, stepping out from behind the counter. "And hopefully, while I'm there, I'll grab a killer, too."

CHAPTER 18

*L*ater that morning, Sarah hopped in her Corolla and headed across town, several miles away, to Hal's Paints. She spotted the giant paintbrush sign and pulled into the establishment's parking lot.

Stepping across the lot, she felt the heat smack her face. If this place were like practically all of the shops in Cascade Cove, it would have its air conditioning cranking.

Entering the store, she removed her sunglasses, allowing her eyes to adjust. The store wasn't brightly lit like most stores. Instead, it was dark, with some display lights over an impressive collection of paints, pencils, and various other mediums that were arranged in a spectrum of colors everywhere.

Across the store, she spotted a man that fit the profile picture Emma had showed her. The man had bright-blue eyes and sported a goatee. His blond hair was pulled back in a ponytail, and his clothing was as colorfully diverse as all of the art supplies around him. To finish off the ensemble, he was wearing sandals, and Sarah cringed internally when she witnessed the white of his ankle socks between the leather straps of his footwear.

Sarah approached the man. "Hi, are you Hal Umberland?"

"Yes, can I help you with something?" His voice was airy, as if he'd been talking through his nose.

"I read online that Abe Dalton sold you a print as an original."

Hal's lips flat-lined. "Did he scam you, too?"

"No, but I'm just curious about how you knew that it was a print, and not an original."

"Believe me, I can tell."

"And you got it directly from him?"

"Sure did. I paid ten grand for that painting!"

"Ten grand?!" Sarah almost choked on her words.

The man crossed his arms. "Yeah. I admit, I bought it without the knowledge of how to know if a painting is authentic or not. Now, I teach classes here at my store on the very subject. Anyone can learn. You want to see the 'painting'?" Hal made air-quotes with both hands when he said "painting."

"You have it here?"

"Yeah, it's in the back." He waved for her to follow him. As he led her toward the back of the store, he said over his shoulder, "I keep it here because it's a good example to teach others how to identify if an art piece is an original or not."

"I see."

The man turned to her as he was walking. "I teach classes every week on it. Like I said, several years ago, when I bought Abe's painting, I didn't know how to tell the difference. It wasn't until one of my colleagues questioned the authenticity of the piece when I showed it to him. He loved the painting, but then he noticed something."

Hal led her into one of the side rooms on the far end of the store. He turned on the lights, illuminating a large room with tables and a white board, set up like a classroom. He continued, "My colleague said the thickness of the paint didn't seem varied like it should. Then he started inspecting it some more."

Sarah waited as the man browsed through a dozen canvases at the corner of the classroom and pulled one out. She could tell immediately from the style that it was a painting done by Abe. It was another ocean piece, but this one was a closeup of the sand and a beautiful seashell of ivory and coral, with the ocean water thinly stretching, as if reaching for the shell. It was a lovely piece of art.

"It looks real to me," Sarah said, stepping closer to study the painting. "It's even on canvas."

"Ah, but if you look closely, you will see it's not real." Hal set the canvas on a table and turned on the overhead lights that were aimed toward the painting. He pointed at the lights. "Natural light bulbs. Just got to wait for them to warm up a bit."

Sarah nodded.

Hal strode over to his desk and pulled out a magnifying glass from the drawer, holding it up. "We'll need this." He walked back to the table where the painting was. "I think the bulbs are warmed up enough. Here." He handed Sarah the magnifying glass. "Take a look."

Sarah took the magnifying glass and leaned closer toward the painting.

Hal continued, "See, it's not just the paint thickness, it's also the variation of texture." He pointed to the mentioned features. "See, the texture is consistent throughout, like a pattern."

Sarah peered through the magnifying glass, and her mouth dropped. "Oh my!" She looked up. "But how?"

Hal grinned, though she could tell it wasn't out of

amusement. "It can easily be done by a photomechanical offset process or giclee printer."

Sarah squinted, peering through the magnifying glass again. "But there are brush strokes, too."

"Yes, and that's what makes Abe's painting seem even more authentic. They used a thick, textured paper that had brushstrokes already pressed into it before the painting was printed. Here"—Hal took the magnifying glass and hovered it over where the water met the sand, and pointed to a specific brushstroke—"you see this brush stroke?"

"Yeah."

"See how it continues from the water into the sand? If this were an original, the brush stroke would stop there, not continue into the sand, because the artist would have to change to a different color of paint."

"So, how does an artist get this done?"

"It's easy. In the past, many art galleries could do this, but today, there are so many companies that will do this for the artist. They can even send their scanned artwork through the company's website or via email, and they will make the print. It's also done on demand and shipped directly to the person paying for the print, rather than to the artist."

"Wow."

"Yeah, but the thing is, most people who buy them

know they are getting a print. But Abe, well, he had ordered the print himself, and he personally delivered this piece to me at a coffee shop, passing it off as the original. And when I called him out for selling a print as the original, he denied it. At first, no one believed me, so I posted pictures online, but Abe said that I must have bought a print from Donna's Art Gallery and was trying to get money out of him, but I never gave up. That was, until the unfortunate tragedy that happened the other night." Hal shook his head. "Needless to say, I became a prime suspect."

"Really? The police were here?"

Hal nodded. "Of course! Everyone knew about the feud between me and Abe. They took me in for questioning, but luckily, I had an alibi. I was on a trip to France with my fiancée, and I had just gotten back the day after his death. All they had to do was call the airport and talk to my fiancée and one of my employees who covered for me that week, and I was off the hook, thank goodness! The man cheated me, yeah, but I consider what happened to him to be a complete tragedy. No one deserves that."

"You're right, nobody does."

Hal nodded, his ponytail bobbing slightly. "I just can't help but wonder if he's just cheated the wrong person this time."

CHAPTER 19

"*H*al was in France?" Emma asked, sitting behind the counter.

Sarah paced back and forth. "Yeah."

"So, now what?"

"I don't know."

Emma tapped on her keyboard, but Sarah paid no attention. Her mind spun as she tried to figure out what to do next.

Misty hopped up onto the counter, purring softly as her tail batted at the back of Emma's laptop.

"Misty, please," Emma said, trying to move the feline away.

Misty meowed—perhaps, like Rugby, she needed a bit more attention than she was receiving.

Suddenly, Misty spotted something at the far end of the boutique and darted away to investigate.

"I don't know about your cat, Em."

Emma chuckled. "Can say the same thing about your dogs."

Sarah stepped toward her cousin. "Say, Emma...what day is it?"

"Uh, it's Wednesday."

"Wait. Fern's sisters—Lily and Rose—leave every Wednesday to go shopping. Maybe we can get Fern alone, talk to her. I know that she might not have anything to do with the murder, but I can sense that Fern knows something."

"Wasn't she at the amusement park the night of the murder?"

"Yeah, according to Fern's sisters. But I think that was to throw me off and make me *think* it was Fern."

"You think Fern's sisters have any motive?"

"We need proof of it, but one theory could be that Lily and Rose conspired to kill their father so they could sell off his original paintings to get out of their supposed 'financial trouble.' Perhaps Fern has been acting so weird because she's itching to tell someone what she knows."

"Wouldn't she just go to the police if that were the case?"

"I don't know. But listen, let's go before we miss our window of opportunity."

"I can't go. I have to watch the shop."

"I need your help, Emma. Let's see if Grandpa can hold down the fort."

Sarah rushed to the front door and opened it, feeling the rush of hot air smack her face. She called out for her grandpa, and the hammering sounds ceased. Moments later, an exhausted-looking Larry walked up to her.

"Yeah?" Larry asked.

"Grandpa, Emma and I need to take care of some-thing. Could you watch the shop?"

"Uh, yeah. Sure. Could use a break anyway. I'd need a few minutes to get washed off."

"Thanks, Grandpa."

Sarah returned to her cousin, grin on her face. "He said he'll do it. Let's go."

Parked across the street from the Daltons' house, Sarah was in her Corolla, sweating her makeup off as she waited. Emma was in the passenger seat, face red from the heat. There were no signs of anyone. She glanced at her phone, and it lit up as she pressed the side button.

Looking at the time, she sighed—they'd been waiting for an hour and a half.

"They should be leaving any minute," Sarah muttered.

Even though she had the windows open, the heat and humidity were still overwhelming.

These sweltering days were suffocating, and she was starting to question if she would even survive them. She pulled her hair up in a ponytail high on top of her head, and she could feel a bead of sweat roll down the back of her neck, sliding down under her tank top.

"Why don't we put up the windows and run the air conditioning?" Emma asked.

"I want to be able to have eyes *and* ears on the place."

"Gotcha."

Moments later, Sarah heard distant chattering that sounded like Lily, and turned to gaze at the Daltons' place, pulling her sunglasses down to get a better view. The two giddy sisters, with their pastel purses hanging from the crooks of their arms, were making their way to their car. Sarah waited, hearing the car start up and the gravel under the tires crunch as they pulled out of the driveway.

Sarah waited a few moments more before she grabbed a small box from the back seat and then she and her cousin got out of the car, making their way across the street toward the front door of the large house. Working to straighten herself up, Sarah felt the same nervousness she'd have if she were knocking on the door of a guy that she liked. But she had to do this. She had to find out what Fern knew. Had to prove to Adam that she could do this. No—she had to prove it to *herself*.

"Okay, so you remember the plan?" Sarah asked.

Emma tapped the side of her forehead. "Got it."

Sarah took a deep breath and rang the doorbell. The faint sound of footsteps grew louder; then, there was a moment of silence. Sarah assumed Fern was looking through the peephole, and tried to remain calm and confident, waiting for the mysterious woman to open the door. After the pop of a metal latch and a click of the lock, the door opened a crack and Sarah could see half of Fern's face behind it.

Feeling the draft of cold air sweep past her, Sarah smiled. "Hi, Fern. I'm Sarah." She put her hand on her chest.

"I know who you are," Fern said flatly, then glanced at Emma. "Who's this?"

"She's my cousin, Emma. Listen, we wanted to stop by and wish you a happy birthday." Sarah held up the box, which was wrapped in fun balloon-print paper and topped with a green bow.

Fern eyed the box, then cracked a smile. "Thank you."

"May we come in?" Sarah asked.

Fern met Sarah's gaze. "Uh, sure." She opened the door wider, allowing Sarah and Emma to come inside.

Sarah felt like this was a big win. For one, the woman had actually spoken. And she'd allowed them to come in without the other two sisters there. Perhaps, Sarah figured, Fern was tight lipped only when her sisters were present. Or maybe her idea to give the woman a birthday gift had paid dividends.

"My sisters won't be back for at least an hour," Fern said, turning her back on Sarah.

"That's okay." Sarah surveyed the room. Everything seemed to always be in its place and sparkling clean. "How are you doing, Fern?"

In the dining room, Fern glanced back at Sarah, then turned to face her. "I'm fine."

"That's good," Sarah said, joining the woman in the dining area. "Oh, here you go." She handed Fern the present, and without saying a word, Fern unwrapped the gift, opened the box, and gazed in at its contents.

"Thanks," Fern said.

A moment of silence lingered between them. Then Sarah spoke up. "Carrot cake cupcakes from Fudderman's. They are incredible."

Fern nodded, then set the box down on the table, picking at a loose thread on her blouse. Sarah wondered why the woman was acting strange again, but she had to get on with their plan.

"Uh, Fern…could I use your bathroom?" Sarah asked.

Fern nodded. "It's down the hall, third door on the left," Fern said, motioning to the hall Sarah had seen the mysterious woman in the few times she had been there before. She recalled how Fern had disappeared into the shadows, and how creepy that had been.

"Thanks," Sarah said, leaving Emma and Fern in the dining room. On her way toward the hallway, she heard her cousin clear her throat and say, "This is a lovely place you have here."

Good, their plan was in motion, and she hoped Emma could keep the woman occupied.

Sarah passed several rooms and spotted the open powder room door. She flicked on the light, but instead of entering, she closed the door loudly enough that Fern might hear. Then she crept down the hall, rounding a corner, and spotted where she remembered the art studio being. She entered the studio, scanning around. It was exactly the same as it had been the last time she was here. Poking around, she didn't spot the series of paintings that she'd seen the prints of. Perhaps they were in another part of the house.

Exiting the studio, she continued along until she found a closed door at the end of the hallway. She turned the knob and the door creaked as it opened. She stepped into the room and saw the outside sunlight pouring through the windows on the opposite side of the huge room, which Sarah figured was a study. There was a mahogany desk and a lot of books, sculptures, and paintings. Sarah stepped over to one of the large paintings hanging on the far wall and studied it.

Something about it was off. Quite literally—it was slightly tilted to one side, as if whoever hung it had done so in haste.

At the painting, Sarah noticed a dark piece of metal behind it. She grabbed both sides of the painting and removed it, resting it up against another section of the wall.

There, on the wall, Sarah eyed the tall, embedded safe.

She wondered why one would need such a tall safe—perhaps for large weapons, or maybe...

"Artwork."

Sarah reached a finger out toward the keypad and hesitated. What in the world could the code be? Typically, these safes used four-digit codes, but she hadn't a clue as to what the code could possibly be.

"Hmm," she muttered, then she quickly punched in a code that some people—the lazy variety—typically used.

"1-2-3-4."

A red light lit up, indicating that it was the wrong code. It didn't surprise her.

"Maybe it has something to do with his artwork..."

She thought that perhaps the four digits could have to do with when he stopped selling his artwork. Maybe something significant happened that year...

"1-9-8-6."

The red light lit again.

"Shoot." Sarah said, scrunching her brows a moment as she considered other options—there were many *possibilities*. Then her eyebrows shot up when another idea came to mind. Today was Fern's birthday—she had just turned forty. She did the mental math and punched in the corresponding four-digit code on the safe.

A green light illuminated, and she heard a click.

"Bingo!"

Sarah pulled the safe open and saw that it was clearly large enough for her to fit in if she wanted to. Her eyes widened when she saw the collection of a dozen or so canvases.

She hoisted out a few of the canvases and sifted through them, realizing they were all paintings that she'd seen before. They were the same ones she'd seen the prints of in Donna's art gallery—the beachside paintings. Sarah leaned closer, remembering what Hal had said. The corners of her mouth ticked up slightly when she spotted telltale signs that the paintings were, indeed, originals and not prints.

Sarah's eyes widened. Picking one of the art pieces up, she studied it. This one was from the view of a pier, one that she was familiar with. She flipped through some more and pulled out another painting, and then another. All of them were Abe's masterpieces. All originals.

Then, she stopped. There, in her hand, was the one with the shell at the edge of the ocean. Her fingers hovered over all the paint mixed together to make up the shell, her mouth open slightly. Was this the original painting that Hal Umberland thought he'd purchased? She studied the painting, and remembered the exact spots where Hal had described the brush strokes continuing into the sand from the water. On this painting, however, the strokes stopped at the point where Abe would have had to change the paint's color.

"Hal paid ten grand for this piece," Sarah muttered, "but he didn't get the original because it's here in my hand."

So, one mystery solved. But she still had yet to see the painting that could provide the motive for the sisters to murder their father. The painting that, if sold, could net them a fortune now that the esteemed artist was deceased.

Putting the painting to the side, she scanned through more of the canvases. Then, she stopped again, spotting an interesting painting that featured four young girls on the beach, very similar to the beachside series. Two of the girls playing in the sand appeared to be around the same age and had light hair. A third girl had very dark hair and was standing off to the right side, watching the light-haired girls as they played. And the fourth girl, who appeared to be much younger than the other three, was sitting off to the left, minding her own business. The youngest had blonde, curly hair that hugged her small head, and Sarah noticed her striking blue eyes that matched the ocean. This was a trait none of the other girls had.

Sarah was certain that the older children in the picture were Lily, Rose, and Fern. They all bore resemblance to their adult-selves. But Sarah couldn't figure out who the blonde girl was. She pulled her phone out, snapping a picture of the painting, then returned to studying it.

"Hmm." She realized that this painting looked a lot like it could have been a part of the beachside series, but she knew she hadn't seen it before. Sarah studied the painting once more, then flipped it over, scanning the back. She knew that, oftentimes, artists would date their paintings, and she hoped that Abe did as well. In short order, she spotted the handwritten date in the lower right-hand corner: "June 1988"

Sarah's eyes went wide when she realized what she was holding. "The June painting."

CHAPTER 20

Sarah returned the June painting to its place within the collection of original Abe Dalton masterpieces and, once all of the rest of the paintings were in place, shut the safe. Then, she hoisted the painting to cover the safe, ensuring that it was slightly off kilter, as she'd found it.

So, the sisters had had the original paintings here at the house all along—they hadn't been sold off, like they'd suggested.

Out of the study, Sarah quietly closed the door behind her. She hoped Emma was still keeping Fern busy; if she were caught snooping around, she could land herself in all sorts of trouble. But still, she knew that in solving a murder, one had to enter into gray areas, like sneaking into private rooms without permission.

Creeping along the hallway, Sarah reached the bathroom and carefully opened the door. Then she flushed the toilet, adding to the illusion that she'd been in there all along. Though she couldn't be sure Fern could actually hear her, she wanted to cover her bases, just in case. She ran the water for a moment, washing her hands, then flicked some of the water on her face. She dried her hands on the towel and left the powder room.

She walked normally out into the dining room, hearing Emma's voice.

"That is so true," Emma was saying, smacking her hand against the table. "Oh, hey, Sarah. You feeling okay? You look a little clammy."

Holding her stomach, Sarah felt some of the water she'd flicked on her face bead up on her forehead. "Sorry it took so long," she said, voice weak, "but I think I ate something bad." This, of course, had been a part of the plan. Taking *forever* in the bathroom had to have some sort of explanation, and it had been Emma's idea to go with this particular detail.

"Did you want to get going?" Emma asked.

Sarah nodded. "Yeah." She shifted her gaze to Fern. "Sorry we have to run."

"Oh, it's no problem," Fern said, rising from her chair to walk them out.

Once they were outside and Fern had closed the door behind them, clicking the lock, Sarah led her cousin away from the house.

"So?" Emma asked expectantly as they reached the car.

"You'll never believe it," Sarah said, opening her car door and getting inside. "I found the original of the painting that Hal paid for."

Emma was in the passenger seat now. "No way! Is that the ten-thousand-dollar one?"

"Yeah. And you'll never guess what else I found…The June painting."

"Wow! That one is worth a fortune, right?"

"Sure is. Enough for them to get out of financial trouble, and even retire, if they wanted. Now, all we have to do is prove they offed him in order to sell those paintings to pay off their debts."

Emma scrunched her face. "But how?"

Sarah started the car, shifted into gear, and pulled away. "That's what we need to figure out."

Back at the boutique, Sarah and Emma relieved their

grandpa so he could return to his work on the float. The store wasn't busy at all, and they were able to discuss their next steps. As they chatted, Sarah glanced over her shoulder and spotted a woman roaming around, wearing sunglasses, a big sun hat, and pink lipstick. She was studying the dog bows, and Sarah was surprised she hadn't heard the woman enter the store.

"Need help finding anything?" Emma called out to the woman.

"Just browsing," the woman said, keeping her focus on the dog bows.

Emma shifted her gaze back to Sarah. "I still can't believe it. We pay Fern a visit and end up finding the original June painting!"

Sarah motioned for her to keep her voice down.

"Sorry," Emma said. "Show me the picture again."

Sarah pulled her cell phone out of her pocket and showed her cousin the picture of the painting.

"Hmm," Emma said. "Four girls..."

"Yeah. Not sure if it's to balance out the painting or—"

"You know, Sarah, that to balance out a painting, you use an odd number of people or objects."

"I guess you're right. So, who do you think this girl is?"

Before Emma could reply, the woman in the sun hat

strolled up to the counter with a stuffed porcupine. She turned to Sarah and smiled. Sarah smiled back and slipped her phone into her pocket.

From behind the counter, Emma said, "Hi, did you find everything okay?"

"Sure did."

Emma eyed the toy. "The porcupine. Nice choice. This toy has a squeaker in it, so be sure to monitor your pup so he doesn't choke on it."

"Thank you. I'll keep an eye on him." Then she turned to Sarah, pushing her sunglasses up the bridge of her nose. "How can something so cute be so dangerous?"

Sarah shrugged. "I don't know."

"Oh," Emma continued, "and I think these toys have little names on their tags." Emma searched the toy for its tag. "Here it is. This is Prickles!"

The woman giggled. "Well, how about that? Simply adorable."

After the woman paid, Emma placed the porcupine in the bag and handed it her. "You have a nice day!"

"You too," the woman said, then she sauntered out of the shop.

Emma stepped over to where Sarah was standing, her voice hushed. "So, how many paintings did you say were in there?"

"I don't know."

"I wonder if he never sold any of his originals."

"That's what I'm figuring. I mean, I don't know for sure, but he has an awful lot of original paintings in there. And it's very suspicious that Lily and Rose said he probably sold a lot of his paintings off."

"That's only to cover their own butts."

Sarah nodded. "Maybe."

Just then, Sarah's phone buzzed in her pocket. She pulled it out and glanced at it. "That's strange."

"What?"

"I have a missed call."

"From who?"

"It's from a number I don't recognize, but they left a message." Sarah tapped on "voicemail" and put her finger up to tell Emma to give her a minute. As she listened to the message, she furrowed her brows.

Once Sarah lowered her phone, Emma asked, "Who was it?"

"Donna."

"From the gallery?"

"Yeah, she says she wants to meet somewhere to talk."

"I wonder what that's about."

Sarah shrugged. "She wants to meet today. I'll call her back and see what this is all about."

CHAPTER 21

*S*arah pulled open the door to Patricia's Tea Room and was greeted by the smell of tea and fresh pastries. She spotted Donna, with her big scarf and red-rimmed glasses. The woman looked up from her cup of tea and waved at Sarah.

Walking up to the table, Sarah eased herself into the chair opposite Donna.

Moments later, a waitress came over to take her order. Sarah realized the woman wasn't anyone she'd met before, and figured Patricia and her granddaughter, who ran the tea room together, were either in the back or were taking the day off.

"What would you like?" the waitress asked Sarah.

Sarah considered getting her favorite, the Boardwalk

Banana Extravaganza, but thought better of it. She was there to have tea and talk, not to stuff a massive banana sundae down her gullet. There was a time for that, and now wasn't that time.

"I'll have the lavender lemon tea with a side biscuit, please," Sarah said.

"Sure thing," the waitress said, then scurried off to retrieve her order.

"So, what did you want to talk about?" Sarah asked Donna.

Donna cleared her throat. "Ever since you came into the gallery asking about Abe's work, I couldn't stop thinking about my relationship with him."

"Your relationship?"

"I didn't tell you the whole truth about Abe."

The waitress returned with Sarah's tea and biscuit, and she couldn't wait for the woman to scamper off so Donna would continue. Once she was gone, Sarah ignored her tea, staying intently focused on Donna. "Oh? So you knew him well?"

"Yeah. We were close when we were young and just starting our careers." Donna took a sip of her tea, then set the cup down, looking at it. She smiled at the memory. "He was an amateur artist, and I was just opening my gallery. We became good friends, helping each other out. I displayed his art, and he drove people to my gallery."

"What happened?"

"Well, I was an exuberant, tough, young woman. They called me 'tough as nails' in the papers. I was all business, so when I opened my gallery, I recognized that I was the only one in the area for miles. Artists didn't have anywhere else to go, really."

"I see. Not a bad position for you to be in."

"Yeah, so being that I was the only game in town, I set it up where I took a fifty percent commission."

Sarah's eyes went wide. "Fifty?"

Donna nodded. "My argument was that I was not only displaying their art, but also setting up the presentation with the best lighting; taking professional photographs for advertising; marketing; and caring for the artwork. And, of course, selling. Most artists don't know how to market their work, nor want to. They simply don't have time for all that. Their job is to create the art. Mine is to sell it."

Sarah took another sip of her tea, waiting for Donna to continue.

"Abe was the first and only artist I ever met who knew anything about selling art," Donna said. "He was smart." She paused. "I'd say brilliant. I made so much money within weeks, and I trusted him. He got a cut of the other artists' commissions. So, things were going along well for a while, until…"

"Until what?"

"Well, let's just say, Abe got me mixed up in some kind of scam in my own gallery."

"Let me guess—selling prints as originals?"

Donna nodded. "Bingo. I confronted him. Told him I would tell everyone about his little scheme. But he said, if I told anyone, he would just tell the whole town that *I* was the one scamming people—passing the artists' prints off as the originals, then pocketing the difference while paying the artists a paltry sum. And who were they going to believe? The 'tough-as-nails' gallery owner who moves into the area to 'exploit artists,' or a poor, beloved local artist who has lived in the area all his life?" Donna paused, clearly holding back her emotions. "He was right. Many locals felt I was taking advantage of artists already."

"So, what did you do?"

"I knew something about him. Something I knew I could hold against him. I told him if he didn't leave, I would tell his wife about his affair."

Sarah gasped. "An affair?"

"Yes. I knew he loved his wife, and he had three little girls. And one thing I knew he would never want to happen would be to tarnish his reputation." Donna reached a hand across the table and took Sarah's hand. "Abe was not a good man, Sarah. He scammed people, he cheated and lied all his life, and he tried to use people like me. What happened to him was horrible, but he crossed so many people—there's a laundry list of them."

The waitress approached the table and set the check between Sarah and Donna. Sarah reached for it, but Donna put her hand over it and slid it toward herself. "I'll get it, Sarah."

"Are you sure? I can pay for my own, at least."

"No, I'm the one who asked you here, and I appreciate your company."

Sarah smiled. "Thank you."

Donna opened her pocketbook. As it flipped open, Sarah spotted a baby picture. As she studied it, something about the girl looked familiar…

"Is that your daughter?" Sarah asked.

Donna glanced down at the picture. "Oh, yes. That's Claire when she was a little girl."

Sarah leaned forward in her chair. "How's she doing?"

"Great," Donna said, taking a final sip of her tea.

"You said she helps you at the gallery?"

"Yeah, she is a brilliant young lady. So smart." Donna wore a proud look on her face.

"I'd like to meet her sometime," Sarah said. "Will she be around later today, or tomorrow?"

"Oh, she is out of town this week. She is taking my place at the National Fine Arts Fair."

"I see. Well, maybe I'll get to meet her soon."

Donna smiled. "I'm sure you will."

CHAPTER 22

Sarah rushed back to the boutique, anxious to tell Emma what she had learned. Outside, Larry and Teek were covering the float, likely to keep their creation from the elements, though she knew it was also to keep everyone in suspense. She quickly waved to them, then opened the door and spilled in. "Emma!"

Hurrying inside, she stopped abruptly. There, in the middle of the boutique, stood Adam, arms crossed.

"Adam, what are you doing here?"

"Came to talk with you. I tried calling you and texting you. You never answered."

"What did you want to talk about?"

"Look, I'm sorry about the other night and how I've

been about you getting involved in the murder investigation. Just, after what happened the last time, I thought about different scenarios. How it could have played out differently. What if I had gotten there a moment later? I got worried."

Sarah let out a long breath. "I'm sorry, too. I shouldn't have bit your head off and called you controlling…and snuck behind your back."

Adam smiled. "I knew you were sleuthing!"

"How could I not?"

Adam leaned closer. "Maybe we can start over?"

Sarah nodded. "Yeah, I think we should."

She knew it wasn't just good for their friendship; they needed to work together if they wanted to nab the killer. One thing was clear in Sarah's mind: a murderer was still out there, and she and Adam needed to bring them to justice.

"Care to compare notes?" Adam asked.

Sarah smiled. "Would love to."

Off behind the counter, Sarah could hear her cousin sigh, and when she glanced over, she was in the middle of shaking her head. Instead of click-clacking on her computer, Emma strolled over, seemingly ready to get down to business.

Sarah filled Adam in on everything she'd learned,

even all that she'd just discovered from Donna about an affair.

"Really?" Adam asked. "I know Abe's wife passed years ago, but I hadn't heard about an affair."

"It was a long time ago. Back when the sisters were kids, apparently."

"Oh."

"What did you find?"

Adam pulled a pad out of his pocket. "Well, we just interviewed the Dalton sisters and a few irate customers of Abe's. One was scammed out of ten grand."

"Hal Umberland. Yeah, I know."

Adam glanced at her, then returned his gaze to his pad. "Could be a motive for murder, though he had no opportunity to kill Abe—he was in France. We checked with the airport, and his alibi is solid."

"I'm assuming you interviewed a lot of the staff at the amusement park?"

"Yeah. Even tracked down the fellow who was working the Ferris wheel that night."

"Pete Melinsky."

"So, I guess you know he's got a solid alibi too."

"Yeah, sick sister."

"Right."

"Anyone else?"

Adam shook his head.

"So that leaves the Dalton sisters," Sarah said.

"Appears that way. Like you said, they have all of his original artwork, and it all just went up in price."

"Yeah, that could help with their financial woes, if what I've heard is true."

"We looked into that," Adam said, raising an eyebrow. "The quiet one, Fern, it turns out, is quite the collector."

"Of what? Art?"

"Not just art but books, antiques, you name it. She has a stash of items that could stock a very large store, if you ask me. A lot of it was purchased on credit—she owes a bundle."

"Are you sure the other sisters aren't in debt too?"

"Fern's name is the only one on these loans, Sarah."

"Hmm," Sarah said, scratching her chin.

"What?"

"Well, Fern's sisters said she was at the amusement park that night. I wonder if she got her hands on a gun..."

Adam let out a sharp breath. "We'd need to get a confession—unless we found the gun that killed Abe and linked it to Fern, I'm afraid that wouldn't be enough to go by."

"But she has motive—tons of debt to pay off with the proceeds of his art. And she has opportunity—she was *there* at the amusement park around the time he was shot!"

"If what her sisters said was true...but we don't know that for sure. We have no proof, Sarah."

Sarah nodded. Adam was right. They had no solid proof that she had killed her father. She stepped past Adam and Emma, straining to think of something. Anything. At a standstill, all she could say was, "I need to walk the dogs or something."

"What?" Emma asked.

"I need to clear my mind. We're not getting anywhere, and I'm just so frustrated."

"I'll go with you," Emma said.

Adam stepped up to Sarah, putting an arm around her shoulder. "Me too."

As if on cue, Rugby and Winston raced by from somewhere in the boutique, both sitting pretty for Sarah.

"They are psychic," Emma said.

"Must be," Sarah said, then grabbed their leashes and put them on.

Larry walked in, and Emma asked, "Could you watch the shop again? We'd like to take the dogs."

Larry shrugged. "Sure, it's the slow time of the day. I'll start prepping for dinner while I watch the store."

"How will you do that?" Emma asked.

"Use my new baby monitor."

"Baby monitor?" Sarah asked.

Larry pointed to a small device by the front door. "It picks up the sound of the bell whenever someone opens the door. And upstairs, I have the 'parent' unit. Now I can get some stuff done up in the apartment, even during business hours, when you girls are out and about."

Sarah laughed. "You never cease to amaze me with what you come up with."

"Wait till the parade," Larry said. "You'll love what Teek and I created."

"Can't wait," Sarah said, then she, Emma, Adam, and the dogs said their goodbyes to Larry, leaving him alone with his baby-monitor-equipped boutique.

Outside, they strode down the main strip, chatting about everything but the murder. Sarah was glad for the change of pace—she needed to clear her mind of all things involving the Abe Dalton case.

Sarah was gripping Winston's leash, and the dog was walking nicely for her, as usual. To her left, Emma was walking Rugby, who was obediently trotting by her side, without a hint of him pulling. And to her right strode Adam, who didn't seem at all disappointed that he wasn't responsible for any creature but himself on this walk.

Down past the Banana Hammock, Sarah was glancing at Adam when she saw a thin woman with jet-black hair and ghostly white skin on the other side of the street.

Sarah elbowed Adam. "Hey, isn't that Fern?"

"Hmm, looks like it."

The ghostly woman was standing at the sidewalk near an alleyway and Sarah noted another woman talking with her, moving her arms wildly as if they were in a heated argument. Sarah couldn't make out who the woman was, as her back was facing the road, but her attire gave her a hint…

"Wait here," Sarah said to Emma.

"What are you doing?" Adam asked.

Sarah stepped into the road, then saw the woman who was talking to Fern turn around. She was wearing a white, sleeveless blouse with a pressed skirt, high heels, and pink lipstick, and Sarah recognized the woman, somehow, but couldn't pinpoint from where.

The woman led Fern between two of the buildings, and then it hit Sarah. A picture flashed in her mind, one she remembered seeing not too long ago, and the woman's identity became crystal clear.

It couldn't be…could it?

But it was!

Sarah's mouth dropped, and she rushed out in the street, ignoring the honking of horns. The people driving would just have to get over her indiscretion. She had a mystery to solve.

CHAPTER 23

*A*cross the street, Sarah realized that she still had Winston trotting at her side. She could hear Adam behind her, asking where she was going. Behind him, on the other side of the street, Emma was yelling at Rugby, who was pulling with all of his might as she held him back from rushing into traffic.

But Sarah ignored all that, and simply focused on going after the two women who'd gone into the alley-way. "I know the woman who's with Fern," was all Sarah could say over her shoulder.

She raced between the buildings where she'd seen them go, and was about to enter the alleyway, when a strong hand landed on her shoulder.

"Sarah, what are you doing?" came Adam's stern voice.

Sarah spun. "I know the woman that's with Fern."

"Who?"

"Wait," Sarah said, shushing him. She crept down the alleyway and could hear a woman's voice growing louder, bouncing off the brick buildings that flanked the alley. The voices were coming from somewhere around the corner at the next intersection, where another small side street was.

"Where's the painting, Fern?" the woman asked. "I know you have it!"

"I don't know what you are talking about," came Fern's reply.

"*The* painting, Fern. The June painting. You have it, and it belongs to me."

Sarah inched closer to the corner, feeling Adam's presence right behind her. Perhaps she'd mistaken the woman's identity. Maybe the woman was another person who Abe had scammed—she'd probably purchased the June painting and had received a print, much like poor Hal Umberland had.

"I don't know what you are talking about," Fern said. "My father never did a June painting."

"Okay, you want to do this the hard way, Fern?"

Sarah heard a gun being cocked. Before Adam could take his own gun out of its holster, Sarah turned to him and handed him Winston's leash. "Hold this."

Adam's voice came out in a harsh whisper: "No, Sarah."

Sarah stepped around the corner, toward the women, revealing herself.

"So, Claire," Sarah said, eyeing the woman in high heels. "I thought you were at the National Fine Arts Fair."

Claire, the woman Sarah only knew as Donna's daughter, kept the gun aimed at Fern. A slight breeze picked up and she saw her blonde hair flutter lightly. "Sarah, the sleuth of Cascade Cove, right? So glad you've decided to join us. I've heard so much about you."

Sarah swallowed hard. How did she know her name? she wondered. Of course—from Donna.

"I know what you're thinking," Claire continued. "But, Sarah, you're too easy. You gave yourself away. You gave everything away. Rule number one of sleuthing: make sure you're not being followed."

"You were following me? For how long?"

"Since the day you stepped foot in my mother's gallery."

"You followed me to the Dalton's house?"

"I followed you everywhere. How do you think I know that Fern, here, has the June painting? I overheard your little sidekick talking all about it. Which brings me to rule number two: don't relay everything you know out in public for others to hear."

Suddenly, the realization smacked Sarah in the face, hard. She remembered the woman in the boutique the other day, the one with the sunhat, the glasses, and the same pink lipstick she was wearing at that very moment. She'd seen the woman in the picture on her mother's desk at the art gallery, yet Sarah hadn't recognized the woman when she was in her grandpa's boutique. Sarah felt like kicking herself for missing that the killer had been hidden in plain sight.

"You were at the boutique and you were eavesdropping on me," Sarah said, staring at the woman.

Claire smiled. "Guess I'm a better sleuth than you."

"And you're trying to steal the June painting. But why?"

"It's not stealing when it's owed to you."

"What do you mean, it was owed to you?"

"You still haven't figured it out, Sarah?"

Sarah tried hard to figure out what Claire was talking about, but she couldn't make sense of it. She shook her head.

Claire dropped her shoulders and raised an eyebrow. "Really?" She paused. "I think Fern, here, even knows what's going on."

Then Sarah thought back to when she had first heard

of Donna's art gallery, when Misty had inadvertently pushed the scrapbook onto the floor. She thought of the first picture of Donna she'd seen, and the little girl on her lap. The blonde, curly hair that hugged the baby's head, and the striking blue eyes.

Sarah's stomach churned when she made the connection: the June painting contained four girls, instead of the three she knew were Abe's daughters. She had wondered about the fourth girl—the one with the same curly blonde hair and blue eyes as the picture in Donna's wallet. She recalled flipping the painting over and finding the date on the back: June 1988. Donna's voice echoed in her mind: "I stopped selling Abe's paintings in 1986." Finally, her memory flipped to the conversation she'd had with Donna at the tea shop, when the woman said that she couldn't stop thinking about her relationship with Abe...Donna's voice echoed again in her head: "He had an affair."

Of course, it all made sense. Claire was the fourth girl in the painting, and the affair Abe had was with none other than...

Sarah's eyes grew wide at the realization, and the words exploded from her mouth: "Abe's your father!"

CHAPTER 24

"Took you long enough to figure it out," Claire said.

Sarah glanced at Fern, and could tell the woman's bottom lip was trembling. Sarah had to think of something, and fast—she needed to get Claire to stop pointing her gun at the poor woman. She knew she needed to be sly in order to pull it off—words over actions, she thought, formulating a plan. Of course, Adam was still in the shadows with Winston, or maybe he was doing his best to keep Emma from entering this dangerous situation. Either way, in order to save Fern and get a full confession out of Claire, Sarah knew it was important that Claire thought Sarah was the only one there.

Claire continued, "Now that everything is out in the open, it's time to hand over what Abe owes me." Claire looked at Fern, and the pale woman's eyes grew wide at the realization that this could be the end of the line for her.

"You mean your *father*," Sarah said.

Claire fixed her gaze on Sarah. "Same difference. It's not like the man was ever in my life. I mean, he did everything in his power to try to hide the fact he even knew me!"

Sarah racked her brain, trying to find any way to get Claire to stop pointing the gun at Fern. "Maybe that's because he knew what you really are."

"And what's that?"

"A cold-hearted murderer."

As the words rolled off Sarah's tongue, she knew they would do the trick of getting Claire to take her aim off of Fern...

...and that's exactly what she did, whipping the gun in Sarah's direction. "Maybe you should go first," Claire said, wearing a smirk. "I'll off you just like I offed my so-called 'father.'"

Suddenly, as if the confession was what he had been waiting for, Adam jumped out from the shadows, gun pointing at Claire and Winston at his side. "Police! Put the gun down and keep your hands where I can see them!"

Claire's eyes darted between Sarah and Adam, and Sarah couldn't help but think he was right—she did put herself in precarious situations.

"Drop the gun, Claire," Adam said, voice firm. "It's over."

Sarah eyed the gun, still fixed on her. Why hadn't she listened to Adam? But then, she would have never gotten a confession.

Hoping beyond hope that the woman would listen to Adam, Sarah grit her teeth. Was this it? Was it the end of the line for *her*, instead of Fern? Would she be Claire's next victim?

Then, Sarah saw it. Claire's hand shook slightly, and she thought that her trigger finger would shake as well.

But it didn't. Instead, Claire's eyes welled up with tears. "No, you don't understand. *He* made me this way. He ignored me—it was like I didn't even exist. Even after he died, you know who got everything?" Claire paused. "His daughters. Except one. Me. He didn't want to be associated with me, even after his death."

Adam inched closer, Winston creeping at his heels. "Just lower the gun, Claire."

Tears were now streaking down her face. "He wouldn't even acknowledge that I was his daughter the night I confronted him at the amusement park. That's why I shot him. I couldn't take it anymore!"

"Drop the gun."

Claire finally dropped the gun and Sarah breathed a sigh of relief.

"Now step away from the weapon. Slowly."

Claire did as she was told, stepping back with her hands now raised in the air.

Adam rushed toward her gun and kicked it aside, then quickly holstered his gun and rushed her, letting go of Winston. Winston trotted over by Sarah's feet, but she couldn't even bring herself to pet him. Instead, she stepped toward Fern, who was visibly shaken. Sarah could relate; she felt the aftereffects of the adrenaline that coursed through her own body.

"Fern, are you all right?" Sarah asked.

Fern nodded, clearly still in shock.

Adam cuffed Claire, then radioed for backup—perhaps Officer Deats or Officer Finley would arrive soon to question all parties involved. Either way, Sarah couldn't wait to go home and wind down. The killer had been nabbed, and all was well in the world.

Sarah let out another sigh of relief and—

"Let my daughter go!" The woman's voice pierced the air, sending Sarah's heart racing again.

Sarah immediately recognized the voice. She

whipped her head around to see Donna in her oversized scarf, signature red-rimmed glasses, and a pistol in her hand. She had both feet planted steady on the ground, aiming the gun at Sarah.

Donna's eyes narrowed and her voice echoed off the buildings: "You are a little troublemaker, aren't you?"

CHAPTER 25

"*D*onna...I..." Sarah stammered as she looked down the barrel of a gun, again.

Donna cut in, "Running around Cascade Cove, stirring things up. Couldn't leave well enough alone, could you?"

"What do you—"

"My daughter is smart and a hard worker—a business lady, like myself. She deserves more. And Abe was a filthy snake, who didn't think about anyone but himself. And I'll be damned if someone like you takes that away from her. So, here's what's going to happen: Mr. Macho Cop, here, is going to let my daughter go. And Fern, here, is going to be a dear and get us that June painting. And you, Sarah, you're going to be our collateral."

"I don't think so, Mrs. Covell," Adam said, placing his hand on his holstered pistol.

Donna grabbed Sarah in one quick swoop and held the gun at her back. Sarah, now facing Adam and Claire, felt the metal pressing into her spine. "Make another move, Officer, and your girlfriend gets it."

Adam motioned to Claire, who was still in front of him. His hand lingered by his pistol, still holstered. "Oh, yeah? I have your daughter."

"You wouldn't," Donna sneered. "You're a cop!"

Adam narrowed his eyes at the woman. "Try me."

Sarah peered around. She spotted Claire's gun still lying on the ground where Adam had kicked it, but there was no way for her to get it—not before getting shot. Then she looked for Winston but couldn't find him —she only used her peripherals, not attempting to move her head to get a better look.

Donna continued, "You hurt my daughter and I'll…"

"You'll do what?" Adam's voice was firm.

Claire cried, "Mom, please!"

"Let my daughter go!" Donna shouted, gripping her pistol even tighter.

Sarah held her breath and felt her pulse beating in her temple—this standoff was becoming too much for her to handle.

She hoped backup would arrive soon. Anyone…

Emma…Winston, even—

A flash of yellow fur, accompanied by a mixture of white and brown, streaked into the alleyway, collar tags jingling, echoing off the buildings.

The cavalry had finally arrived!

Donna spun around, releasing Sarah slightly from her grip, and screamed as the massive, eighty-pound yellow lab charged at her, knocking her over. Her red-rimmed glasses went flying, along with the gun, which had flung from her hand and flew into the air, though Sarah didn't see where it landed. Rugby reversed course, trotting over to the fallen woman, and his large tongue lapped at the side of her face and hair, getting drool in her dirty-blonde locks.

Winston grabbed at Donna's ankle as Sarah pulled herself from the woman's grip and charged for Claire's gun, lying only a few feet away. Snatching the gun, Sarah whipped it around and took aim at Donna. She half-expected the woman to be nearing her own gun, but she was still lying on the ground with Rugby on top of her, licking her face, gun sprawled several feet from her hand.

Sarah hurried over to where Donna's pistol lay and kicked it toward Adam.

"Nice work, Rugby," Adam said, retrieving the gun. "And you too, Miss Shores."

CHAPTER 26

*S*arah's heartbeat had finally returned to its normal pace, and she spotted Officer Deats lumbering into the alley. She noted white donut powder on the corners of his mouth—apparently, Adam had interrupted his favorite part of the day.

Both Claire and her mother, Donna, were cuffed and ready to be carted off to the station.

"Wait till I speak with my lawyer!" Donna was shouting.

Adam shook his head, leading her toward Officer Deats. "Well, I count three witnesses that heard your daughter admit to the murder of Abraham Dalton, not to mention you obstructing justice. Oh, and the collusion scheme so you could get your hands on his original paintings."

Officer Deats took over, leading Donna out of the alley, and the woman pulled herself away from the man several times as they walked out toward the main street.

Claire was being escorted by Adam, and she glanced back at Sarah and Fern, tears still filling her eyes.

"She'll be going away for a long time for what she did to your father," Sarah said to Fern.

Fern nodded, then put her head against Sarah's shoulder. Sarah put an arm around the woman, consoling her.

"Thank you, Sarah," Fern said. "For everything. If you hadn't come when you did…"

"You're welcome, Fern."

Walking out of the alleyway together, with Rugby and Winston flanking them, Fern said, "Please don't think differently about my father."

"What do you mean?"

"About the affair. I learned about it when I was younger—I overheard my father talking to Donna; they didn't see me. Then, later, I confronted him. He denied it at first, but then he broke down and told me everything. Told me about Claire. Even showed me the June painting."

"Your sisters didn't know?"

"No, and they always wondered why I kept quiet. I was afraid if I talked too much, I would break down like my father did, and end up telling them things that would crush them. Rose and Lily aren't as strong as I am. They are delicate, like the flowers they're named after."

They reached the main street and Sarah felt the sunshine on her face, a welcome feeling after another near-death experience.

Fern continued, "They don't even know that the original paintings are stored away—somewhere where nobody would find them. I never told them about it, since I knew Claire was out there, scheming, and might try to pry the information out of them. So, they were oblivious. I just can't believe it, though…that Claire would do such a thing."

"I can't understand it, either."

Fern nodded. "I suppose not having a father, and being pushed out of his life, would be very difficult to handle."

"I agree, but it's still no excuse."

Fern let out a sigh, and she met eyes with Sarah. "I'm just glad all of this is over."

The following afternoon, Sarah and Emma were sitting at the dining room table in the Daltons' house, having Darjeeling black tea with Rose, Lily, and Fern.

Rose took another sip of her tea and smiled at Emma and Sarah in turn.

"Thanks for inviting us over," Sarah said to the sisters.

"Well," Rose said, "we can't thank you enough for saving Fern's life and getting those awful women where they belong—behind bars."

"It's the least we could do," Sarah said.

Next to her, Emma took a sip of her tea. "Mmm."

"Glad you're enjoying the tea, Emma," Fern said.

Emma said, "It's very good."

"You've never had this kind of tea before?"

Emma shook her head.

"Note the mild spiciness of the tea," Lily said, spreading butter on a biscuit, followed by strawberry jam. "And the jam should complement the biscuits and black tea very well. We're very particular with our pairings."

"Ahh," Emma said, though Sarah knew she had no idea what any of that meant. Neither did Sarah, though she did enjoy a cup of tea from time to time at Patricia's Tea Room.

"Well, we're just glad that things are better now," Rose said. "The three of us had a nice, long chat."

"Oh yeah?" Sarah asked.

"Uh-huh," Fern said. "I told them all about our father."

"We still love Daddy, though," Lily said.

"Yeah," Rose chimed in, "he's still our father, and was a very talented man. Fern even told us about his 'scandal,' which she'd kept from us to protect us. All the things he had done, it's hard to believe, yet I know deep down he was a kind man."

Sarah nodded.

"And the hate mail made more sense after learning all of that," Lily said. "We had no clue why anyone would send such things to him, so we protected him by getting the mail and hiding the offending letters. It was mostly from people claiming that they were being cheated by our father, though we took it entirely a different way."

Rose took a sip of tea, then added, "Yeah. We thought he started doing commissions, and was delivering his own stylistic interpretation of what the client wanted, instead of a literal interpretation."

"Why did you keep them from him?" Sarah asked.

"We didn't want him to be negatively affected. We knew that if he did commissions, it wasn't a major focus. And he didn't often deal with clients, as he was more of an introvert. We wanted to protect him."

"I see," Sarah said, and it became clear why Rose had squashed any talk of the hate mail the two times Lily had tried to bring it up. She was the one focused on protecting their father, while Fern was focused on protecting both her father *and* her sisters.

"Yeah," Fern said, "but now that Claire and her mom are behind bars and aren't trying to get their hands on our father's paintings, I told my sisters about the originals."

"We were so shocked," Rose said. "We thought he'd sold them. But they were here all along, and he'd only told Fern about them. I guess he knew that Fern is like him—quiet—so they would be well protected if anything happened to him. Anyway, they are stunning."

"Wow," Sarah said, "I'd love to see them sometime." Of course, she'd already seen them, using Fern's birthday as the code to gain access to a large safe in Abe's study. But she was glad to hear that Fern had finally let her sisters know of their existence.

"You'll be able to see them soon enough," Lily said. "We're going to do a pop-up exhibit in town and display all of Daddy's artwork. We'll also be selling prints."

"I can't wait," Sarah said, nibbling on her biscuit, then taking a sip of tea.

Fern set her cup down in its saucer, making a *clink* noise, then said, "Excuse me," rising from her seat at the table.

Sarah watched as she strode around the corner, the

same one she'd seen the woman looming at, shrouded in shadows. The once-mysterious woman had just been misunderstood—looks were quite deceiving.

Eating the last of her biscuit, Sarah sipped at her tea. Then, Fern returned, holding a large gift bag.

"Here," Fern said, placing the bag between Sarah and Emma. "This is for you and your family—a symbol of our appreciation."

Sarah reached a hand into the bag and pulled out the framed painting. "Oh my," she said, gawking at the artwork.

Emma leaned closer, eyeing the painting: "Wait, is this of…"

"Your grandpa's boutique," Fern said, nodding. "That's one of his paintings that's part of a series of Cascade Cove's most treasured establishments—your family has definitely added a bit of flare to the area, so much so that my father took inspiration in it. I'm not sure if your grandpa told you, but we used to have a yellow lab, and so our father used to stop by and see Larry all the time. He always enjoyed going there."

"Thank you so much," Sarah said, shifting her gaze between all three sisters. "All of you."

"It's the least we can do for everything you've done. Oh, and in case you're wondering, it's not a print," Fern said. "It's the original."

Chuckles were shared all around the table. They spent the rest of the afternoon sharing stories of their childhoods and of other interesting tales of their lives. Sarah felt she might have some new friends here, people she could share good times with as she spent the rest of her summer in Cascade Cove.

CHAPTER 27

The next day, Adam and Sarah walked along the main strip of Cascade Cove, weaving through some of the crowds. Sarah had Winston with her on a leash, though he didn't really need a lead—he always trotted right beside her, but with the crowds on the boardwalk and now in the street for the parade, she used the leash as a precaution.

She took a deep breath of the warm, salty air, and was grateful that the murder mystery had finally been solved and the perps had been brought to justice.

"I've never seen the parade so crowded before," Adam said. "You think everyone is celebrating the fact that we got more baddies off the streets?"

Before Sarah could conjure up a reply, she spotted

Emma and Mark waving at them. "There they are," Sarah said to Adam.

They strolled over, and Mark and Emma had an extra two chairs for them. Emma was also carrying a huge bag filled with snacks and various types of sunscreen; Mark held a cooler filled with tons of ice and water and some popsicles.

"Wow, you guys really went all out," Sarah said.

Mark said, "I go to this parade every year, and every year it's during a heat wave."

Emma peered around. "I hope this spot is okay. I know it's at the ending point of the parade, but it's jam-packed up that way," she said, motioning down the road.

"This is fine," Sarah said.

Sarah and Adam took their seats and they watched as the parade started. There were various floats—more than Sarah had expected—from different businesses in the area, like Fudderman's and Patricia's Tea Room; even Dunham Vineyards had a float. There were balloons of all shapes and colors, streamers, and people in fun outfits.

There was even a marching band and color guard, and the sound of cheers and merriment filled the air as the large band marched by, playing a rendition of "Wild Thing." Some people even sung along as the trumpets, clarinets, alto saxophones, and flutes played the melody above the tenor saxophones, trombones, and tuba players who carried the bass line. At the rear of the band was the drum line, and Sarah marveled at the bass drums of various sizes, the snare-drummers doing wild tricks—such as using their sticks against a neighboring drum. And then there were the quad players, not to mention the cymbals.

She could see Adam's brow scrunch downward as he plugged both ears with his fingers to avoid the crashing cymbals.

"Here they come!" Emma called out above the sounds of the fading tune.

All four of them rose from their chairs, waving and cheering as Larry's float came into view. Finally, after all of this time, Sarah would see her grandpa's creation come to life.

"Oh my," Sarah shouted, pointing. "Look at that!"

Sarah marveled at the float, which was a large yellow lab that looked similar to Rugby, with sunglasses on and a Hawaiian shirt that matched Larry's. The giant dog was on a surfboard that slid back and forth on a wave. Clearly, this had been a collaboration between the surfer dude and her Hawaiian-shirt-wearing Grandpa. She smiled when she saw the "Larry's Pet Boutique" lettering on the side of the float.

"Wow," Emma said. "I'm impressed."

"Me too," Sarah said. "Looks just like Rugby."

And there, in all of his glory, Sarah spotted her grandpa standing at the front corner of the float, waving and smiling. Rugby was sitting at the other corner, wearing one of Larry's Hawaiian shirts and sunglasses to match the over-sized, surfing dog. And a shirtless Teek stood next to him, holding his leash, his puka shell necklace bright against his tanned chest.

Glancing at Adam, Sarah witnessed the most epic eye-roll as he crossed his arms. Adam grimaced. "Does that guy ever wear a shirt?"

Sarah nudged him. "Would you wear a shirt if you had a chest like that?"

"Who says I don't?"

Sarah laughed, and moments later, the float was almost right in front of them, when Sarah noticed Rugby seemingly distracted by something. Then she saw a butterfly fluttering around his nose.

"Uh, what's going on with Rugby?" Emma asked.

"It's a butterfly." Mark pointed.

Suddenly, the butterfly fluttered away, though apparently Rugby wasn't done marveling at it. He pulled on the leash hard, lunging off the float, pulling poor Teek behind him. Larry followed closely behind, abandoning the float to chase after them, yelling and waving his arms. Rugby veered away from the crowd, rushing toward the drum line at the rear of the marching band.

"Oh no!" Sarah cried, about to rush after her yellow lab. If history were any indication, she knew that Rugby was about to slam into one of the unwitting percussionists, much like he'd slammed into the back of Larry's chair during dinner. Only, this time, a forkful of shrimp scampi wouldn't go flying—an entire drum section would go cascading across the street.

But before she could will her legs to work, she heard Teek's sharp voice cut through the noise. "Rugby!" the surfer dude said. "Halt!"

Rugby screeched to a halt and spun around, his tongue flopping lazily out of his mouth as he trotted back toward Teek obediently.

"Wow," Emma said in awe. "Look at that. Teek's amazing."

"It was just luck," Adam said, crossing his arms. "Coincidence."

But Sarah knew it wasn't a coincidence. Teek definitely had a way about him when it came to working with animals, and she'd have to get some pointers off of him real soon.

Moments later, she watched as Teek and Larry guided Rugby back to the float to continue on the parade route. The crowd cheered at Teek, who took a bow, and waved back at them. He'd saved the day in his own right, the hero of the day.

The Larry's Pawfect Boutique float rolled along until it was out of sight. Sarah leaned in closer to Adam, who put his arm around her. They sat in a blissful calm as the festivities continued around them. Soon, she'd have to leave. Or would she?

It was suddenly clear to Sarah that a decision had to be made.

CHAPTER 28

A few days later, after Grandma had returned from working on the cruise, they were all gathered around the last available table at Ahoysters. Sarah scanned the table, and saw her grandpa nuzzling up to Grandma. She'd only been away a short time, and yet, he seemed to miss her tremendously. Next to the two lovebirds was Emma, who'd brought Mark along for his second outing to the new restaurant. And next to Mark was Adam, who was looking around in amazement at all of the pirate-themed memorabilia on the walls.

"So glad you came," Grandma said to him. "I missed you."

"Glad to be here," Adam said.

"Is this your first time at Ahoysters?" Mark asked.

"Uh-huh," Adam said, holding up the ancient-looking menu, studying it. "Clams by the bucket...hmm."

Suddenly, the spry young man in the pirate garb, who Sarah remembered from the last time she had been there, came up behind Adam. "Yarrrrr!!!"

Adam's body jetted a few inches off the chair and his menu flung from his hands, landing on the lit candle in the middle of the table. The menu quickly caught fire, and the server shouted, without any pirate dialect this time, "Oh, geez, not again!" He grabbed the menu and shook it a few times, and the flames quickly extinguished.

"Sorry about that," Adam said.

"Yarrr! Not a problem, matey."

"Tell me," Adam said, turning around, "do you have to say 'yarr' all day long?"

The man in the pirate outfit leaned closer to Adam, losing his pirate accent once again. "Yeah, I do...but I have to say, the tips from all the generous tourists make up for it."

"Looks like you've found the *sunken treasure* then," Adam said, attempting a bit of humor.

Mark coughed, and Emma shook her head.

Sarah started to chuckle, though it was somewhat delayed

"At least someone gets the joke," Adam said, nudging Sarah.

"Yeah," Sarah said. "Ha."

"Not a bad joke at all," the waiter said. "Blackbeard would indeed be proud! Yarr!!"

Sarah couldn't tell if the waiter was being sincere, or if he was just buttering poor Adam up to increase his tip intake. She knew it wasn't treasure the man *found* at the end of the night, but his nightly take was a result of hard work, sweat, and a heaping serving of pirate dialect.

The man took their orders, and Sarah's stomach rumbled. She couldn't wait to dig into the Seafood Bouillabaisse, which was a mixture of lobster, shrimp, scallops, haddock, mussels, clams, and crab meat in a light marinara sauce of shells.

"So, I still can't believe it was the art gallery owner's daughter," Grandma said.

Sarah nodded. "And her mother was in on the scheme to steal his paintings."

"How shameful. And I can't believe they were aiming guns at you, Adam, and poor Fern. I hope the Dalton sisters are okay."

"They are. We had tea the other day, and you saw the painting."

Larry's grin grew wide. "I've already gotten a dozen compliments about that masterpiece."

Sarah glanced at her grandpa. He had proudly hung up the painting in the boutique, though he took it off the wall every night and stored it in his bedroom, up in the apartment. Even when he took a break, he'd take it along. It was like he and the painting were inseparable.

"I'm just glad all of that is over," Grandma said. "Now Cascade Cove can get back to normal."

Sarah wondered what "normal" even was now for the small beachside town. When she'd first arrived, there was a drowning, and she hadn't thought anything of it. Once it was confirmed to be a murder, she figured it was an anomaly. But then, a second murder occurred —this time a strangling. Still, she didn't think the trend would continue. With this third murder, a trend had begun, and it worried her. If she weren't there to help Adam and his crew, then where would they be in these murder investigations? A shudder went down her spine at the thought that all three crimes would have gone unsolved and the perps would still be on the streets.

Of course, that wouldn't have happened. Adam was skilled, as were his colleagues. They were fine men and women, more than capable of nabbing the bad guys. But she couldn't help but wonder if them having a person like her—who blended in and was able to talk with people without them feeling threatened—was a vital part to them apprehending the killers so quickly. If she left to go back to New York City, and the body count kept rising, would they be able to cope with the influx?

Sarah mulled over those thoughts for a moment, then felt a nudge.

"Earth to Sarah," Adam said, smiling.

"Oh, sorry," she said. "Just got lost in thought."

"About what?"

Before Sarah could reply, she heard her cousin's voice: "So how was your cruise, Grandma? I'm sure it wasn't as exciting as what happened here."

"Most certainly not," Grandma said with a bat of her hand. "Those cruises are a snooze-fest compared to what goes on in Cascade Cove."

Sarah couldn't tell if her grandma was being truthful. Something about her lack of eye contact with anyone when she spoke told Sarah there was more there than met the eye. Certainly, there weren't any *murders* aboard the cruise ship on which Grandma worked. Though, Sarah knew she'd have to ask her about it sometime—or perhaps take her grandma up on the offer to go on a cruise with her when she wasn't working.

"Hopefully things get better here," Emma said.

"Hopefully," a few said in unison, nodding.

Emma turned to Sarah. "So, Sarah, any thoughts on what we talked about?"

Sarah knew what she'd meant—the big question that

everyone at the table probably had. Would Sarah stay or would she go?

For a moment, she thought of the harsh winters up north. The hustle and bustle. The traffic. Those were all things she wouldn't miss. And then there was her career. She loved teaching, though in her mind, she knew she loved being in Florida, working and living with her family. Her grandpa's business was booming now, especially with online sales, and Sarah wanted to be a part of that action. She wanted to help him grow his brand, and work alongside her cousin as they helped get his new line of products in pet stores across the country.

And, of course, there was Adam.

She glanced at him and smiled, studying his brown eyes. He was an amazing person, who she was grateful to have in her life. She wondered what her life would be like with him as a regular fixture.

She wanted to be here with him, with her family, and with the wonderful people of Cascade Cove.

She let out of along breath, and said, "Well..."

Scanning the table, she saw Grandma and Grandpa, Emma and Mark, and Adam. A moment later, the guy in the pirate garb was there too, waiting for her reply.

"Well?" came Emma's voice.

"What are we talking about?" Larry asked, scratching

his head. Grandma whispered something in his ear, and he nodded. "Ah."

Sarah cleared her throat. "I've decided…that I want to stay in Cascade Cove."

Emma shot up out of her chair and came over to Sarah, hugging her. "We're going to have so much fun!"

Grandma clapped her hands together. "Get the wine, Lawrence. We need to toast!"

Adam put his arm around Sarah, gazing into her eyes. "I'm so glad you're staying."

He hugged her and she felt his muscles flex slightly. A tingle of excitement coursed through her body as they embraced, and when they started to loosen their embrace, he gave her a tender kiss on the cheek.

"Aww," Emma said. "Two love birds."

Sarah smirked. "Oh, c'mon. Look at you two."

Emma nuzzled up against Mark but remained silent. Sarah knew that those two were quite the item, much like her and Adam were becoming.

Larry cleared his throat, and wine was poured all around—Dunham Vineyards, of course.

"So, I'd like to make a toast," Larry said, holding his glass up.

Everyone else held up their filled glasses.

Larry continued, "To my wonderful granddaughters, for everything they do. I wouldn't be as happy as I am without them in my life." He set his eyes on Sarah. "And now, to hear that you're staying, it just…it…"

"Grandpa," Emma said, leaning forward, "are you…crying?"

Larry pulled a hanky from his pocket and dabbed his eyes, pushing his glasses up slightly in the process. He pocketed his hanky, and continued, "I'm okay. I'm just so thrilled that you're staying. So, here's to family, and the love and joy that we bring each other!"

Glasses clinked together. "Here, here!"

"Yarrr!" came the server's cry of approval.

A few other patrons clinked their glasses together, as if they'd listened in on Larry's toast.

Sarah took a sip of her wine, savoring the flavor. She also savored the wonderful feeling she had being in Cascade Cove with the ones she loved. She couldn't wait for all the adventures and excitement that awaited her. She was finally home.

# # #

Thank you for reading! Want to help out?

Reviews are a big help for independent authors like me, so if you liked my book, **please consider leaving a review today**.

Thank you!

-Mel McCoy

ABOUT THE AUTHOR

Mel McCoy has had a lifelong love of mysteries of all kinds. Reading everything from Nancy Drew to the Miss Marple series and obsessed with shows like *Murder, She Wrote*, her love of the genre has never wavered.

Now she is hoping to spread her love of mysteries through her new Whodunit Pet Cozy Mystery Series. Centered around a cozy beachside town, the series features a cast of interesting characters and their pets, along with antiques, crafts such as knitting, and plenty of culinary delights.

Mel lives with her two dogs, a rambunctious and bossy Yorkie named Peanut, and a dopey, lazy hound (who snores a lot!) named Murph.

For more info on Mel McCoy's cozy mystery series, please visit: www.melmccoybooks.com

Connect with Mel:

Facebook: facebook.com/CozyMysteryMel
Twitter: twitter.com/CozyMysteryMel

WANT A FREE STORY?

Grab your free copy of *The Case of the Ominous Corgi*, a short cozy mystery featuring Rugby, Winston, and Misty. Simply visit www.melmccoybooks.com and click the "Free Story" link.

59789803R00119